Dear Reader,

Welcome to *Amelia,* another tale in the series of *Great Lakes Romances®,* historical fiction full of love and adventure set in bygone days in the region known as Great Lakes Country.

Like the other books in this series, *Amelia* offers readers the pleasure of a tale skillfully told without the use of explicit sex, offensive language, or gratuitous violence.

We are certain that readers will love *Amelia,* first published 95 years ago, for its light, breezy style, charming illustrations, and revealing glimpses into the attitudes of turn-of-the-century women regarding the question of women's suffrage. We invite you to share your opinion with us by filling out and sending in the survey form at the back of the book.

Thank you for being a part of *Great Lakes Romances®!*

Sincerely,

The Publishers

P.S. Editor Donna Winters, who is also the author of several books in the series, would love to hear from you. You can write to her at P.O. Box 177, Caledonia, MI 49316.

Introduction

At the turn of the century, before all women in America were granted the right to vote by our Federal Government, the women's suffrage question came often before legislators at the state level. *Amelia* explores a fictional example of this process in the State of Illinois where in 1901 and 1903 the question came before the House and Senate on several occasions. (Unlike today, state legislators of that era met only in odd number years, convening on the first Monday in January and adjourning by the first Monday in May.) The fictional reason for the failure of these bills has not been substantiated in truth, but offers a unique perspective on opposing opinions of turn-of-the-century women regarding involvement in politics.

Amelia

Brand Whitlock
Edited by
Donna Winters

Great Lakes Romances®
Bigwater Publishing
Caledonia, Michigan

A special thanks to Tom Huber of the Illinois State Library, Public Services Section/Reference, for research regarding the women's suffrage question in the Illinois House and Senate, 1901-1903.

Amelia
Great Lakes Romances® Encore Edition #2
Copyright c 1999 by Donna Winters, including front and back matter and editorial and illustrative changes to the original material

First Published 1904 as
Her Infinite Variety
The Bobbs-Merrill Company, Indianapolis

Great Lakes Romances® is a trademark of
Bigwater Publishing
P.O. Box 177
Caledonia, Michigan 49316

Library of Congress Catalog Card Number: 99-94634
ISBN 0-923048-88-x

Printed in the United States of America

99 00 01 02 03 04 05 06 /   / 10 9 8 7 6 5 4 3 2 1

Amelia

I

AMELIA came running eagerly down the wide stairs, and though she was smiling with the joy of Morley's coming, she stopped on the bottom step long enough to shake out the skirt of the new spring gown she wore, with a manner that told she had it on that evening for the first time. Morley Vernon hastened to meet her, and it was not until he had kissed her and released her from his embrace that she saw the dressing-case he had set down in the hall.

1

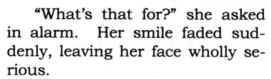

"What's that for?" she asked in alarm. Her smile faded suddenly, leaving her face wholly serious.

"I have to go back tonight," he replied, almost guiltily.

"Tonight!"

"Yes. I must be in Springfield in the morning."

"But what about the dinner?"

"Well," he began, helplessly, "I guess you'll have to get somebody in my place."

Amelia stopped and looked at him in amazement.

"I thought the Senate never met Mondays until five o'clock in the afternoon!"

"It doesn't, usually, but I had a telegram from Porter an hour ago. There's to be a conference in the morning."

2

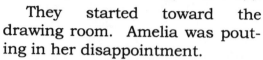

They started toward the drawing room. Amelia was pouting in her disappointment.

"I knew something would spoil it," she said, fatalistically. And then she added, "I thought that Monday afternoon session never lasted longer than a minute. You never went down before until Monday night."

"I know, dear," said Morley, apologetically, "but now that the session is nearing its close, we're busier than we have been."

"Can't you wire Mr. Porter and get him to let you off?" she asked.

Morley laughed. "He isn't my master."

"Well, he acts like it," she retorted, and then as if she had suddenly hit upon an unanswerable argument she went on. "If that's so, why do you pay any attention to his telegram?"

4

"It isn't he, dear," Morley explained, "it's the party. We are to have a very important conference to consider a situation that has just arisen. I must not miss it."

"Well, it ruins my dinner, that's all," she said helplessly. "I wanted you here."

Morley had come up from Springfield as usual for the week's end adjournment, and Amelia had counted on his waiting over, as he always did, for the Monday night train, before going back to his duties in the Senate. More than all, she had counted on him for a dinner she had arranged for Monday evening.

"What time does your train leave?" she asked, in the voice of one who succumbs finally to a hopeless situation.

"Eleven twenty," he said. "But I brought my luggage over with

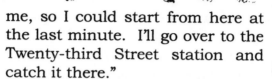

me, so I could start from here at the last minute. I'll go over to the Twenty-third Street station and catch it there."

Amelia had had the deep chair Morley liked so well wheeled into the mellow circle of the light that fell from a tall lamp. The lamp gave the only light in the room, and the room appeared vast in the dimness; an effect somehow aided by the chill that was on it, as if the fires of the Ansley house had been allowed to die down in an eager pretense of spring. It was spring, but spring in Chicago. Sunday morning had been bright and the lake had sparkled blue in the warm wind that came up somewhere from the southwest, but by night the wind had wheeled around, and the lake resumed its normal cold and menacing mood. As Morley sank into

6

the chair he caught a narrow glimpse of the boulevard between the curtains of the large window. In the brilliant light of a street lamp he could see a cold rain slanting down onto the asphalt.

"How much longer is this legislature to last, anyway?" Amelia demanded as she arranged herself in the low chair before him.

"Three weeks."

"Three—weeks—more?" Amelia drew the words out.

"Yes, only three weeks. And then we adjourn *sine die*. The joint resolution fixes the date for June second."

Amelia said nothing. She was usually disturbed when Morley began to speak of his joint resolutions. Which was perhaps, the reason why he spoke of them so seldom.

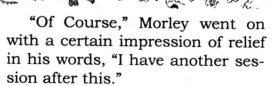

"Of Course," Morley went on with a certain impression of relief in his words, "I have another session after this."

"When will that be?" Amelia asked.

"Winter after next. The governor, though, may call a special session to deal with the revenue question. That would take us all back there again next winter."

"Next winter!" she cried, leaning over in alarm. "Do you mean you'll have to be away all next winter, too?"

The significance of her tone was sweet to Morley, and he raised himself to take her hands in his.

"You could be with me then, dearest," he said softly.

"In Springfield?" she asked incredulously.

"Why not? Some members have their wives with them," he asserted, secretly admitting that only a few members cared to have their wives with them during the session.

"What could one do in Springfield, pray?" Amelia demanded. "Go to the legislative hops, I suppose? And dance reels with farmers and West Side politicians!" She almost sniffed her disgust.

"Why, dearest," Morley pleaded, "you do them a great injustice. Some of them are really of the best people. The society in Springfield is excellent. At the governor's reception at the mansion the other night—"

"Now, Morley," Amelia said with a smile that was intended to reproach him mildly for this attempt to impose upon her credulity.

9

"And besides," Morley hurried on, suddenly taking a different course with her, "you could be a great help to me. I never address the Senate that I don't think of you, and wish you were there to hear me."

"I should like to hear you," said Amelia, softening a little. "But of course I couldn't think of appearing in the Senate."

"Why not? Ladies often appear there."

"Yes, overdressed, no doubt."

"Well, you wouldn't have to be overdressed," Morley retorted. He seemed to have the advantage, but he decided to forego it. He sank back on the cushions of his chair, folding his hands and plainly taking the rest a senator needs after his legislative labors.

"Of course," he said, "we needn't discuss it now. The gov-

10

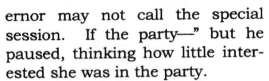

ernor may not call the special
session. If the party—" but he
paused, thinking how little interested she was in the party.

"I wish you'd let politics alone,"
Amelia went on relentlessly. "It
seems so—so common. I don't
see what there is in it to attract
you. And how am I ever going to
explain your absence to those
people tomorrow night? Tell them
that *politics* detained you, I suppose?" She looked at him severely, and yet triumphantly, as if
she had reduced the problem to
an absurdity.

"Why," said Morley, "you can
tell them that I was called suddenly to Springfield— that an important matter in the Senate—"

"The Senate!" Amelia sneered.

"But dearest," Morley began,
leaning over in an attitude for argument.

11

She cut him short. "Morley, do you think I'd ever let on to those Eltons that I *know* anyone in *politics?*"

"Don't they have politics in New York?"

"They won't even know where Springfield is!"

"What'll they say when they receive our cards next fall?" he asked with a smile.

"You needn't think your name will be engraved on them as *Senator*, I can assure you!" Her dark eyes flashed.

Morley laughed again, and Amelia went on.

"You can laugh, but I really believe you would if I'd let you!"

They were silent after that, and Amelia sat with her elbow on the arm of her chair, her chin in her hand, meditating gloomily on her ruined dinner.

13

"If you did any good by being in politics . . ." she paused, thinking, "but I fail to see what good you do." She lifted her head suddenly and challenged him with a high look. "What good *do* you do?"

He spread his hands wide and offered a gentle rejoinder. "If you don't care enough to look in the newspapers—"

"How could I, Morley?" she asked innocently. "How was I to know where to look?"

"In the Springfield dispatches," he answered without rancor, "but the most important work in the legislature isn't done in the newspapers." He rushed on to hide his inconsistency. "There are committee meetings, and conferences and caucuses. That's where policies are mapped out and legislation framed."

He spoke darkly, as of secret sessions held at night on the upper floors of hotels, attended only by those who had received whispered invitations.

"But if you must be in politics," she said, "why don't you do something big, something great, something to make a stir? Show your friends that you are really accomplishing something!"

Amelia sat erect and gave a strenuous gesture with one of her little fists clenched. Her dark eyes showed the excitement of ambition. But Morley drooped and placed his hand wearily to his brow. Instantly Amelia started up from her chair.

"Does that light annoy you?" Her tone was altogether different from her ambitious one. She was stretching out a hand toward the lamp, and the white flesh glowed

15

red between her fingers, held against the light. He was tempted to take it in his own, caress it, and speak again of her joining him in Springfield, but he restrained himself, saying instead, "Never mind the light, it doesn't bother me."

But Amelia rose and twisted the shade of the lamp about, and then, as she was taking her seat again, she went on.

"I suppose it'll be worse than ever after—after we're married." She faltered and blushed and began making little pleats in her handkerchief, studying the effect with a sidewise turn of her head.

Morley bent over, this time taking both of her hands in his.

"If only it were Washington," she bemoaned.

"It shall be Washington, dear," he promised with a squeeze.

16

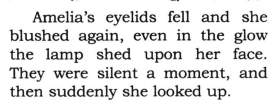

Amelia's eyelids fell and she blushed again, even in the glow the lamp shed upon her face. They were silent a moment, and then suddenly she looked up.

"Washington would be ever so much better, Morley. I should feel as if that really amounted to something. We'd know all the diplomats, and I'm sure in that atmosphere you would become a great man."

"I will, dear. I will, but it will all be for you."

II

WHEN Morley went into the Senate that Tuesday morning and saw the red rose lying on his desk he smiled, and picking it up, raised it eagerly to his face. But when he glanced about the chamber and saw that a rose lay on every other desk, his smile was suddenly lost in a stare of amazement. Once or twice, perhaps, flowers had been placed by constituents on the desks of certain senators, but never had a floral distribution, at once so modest and impartial, been made before. Several senators, already in their seats, saw the check this impartiality gave Morley's vanity, and they laughed. Their laughter was of a tone with the tinkle of the crystal prisms of the chandeliers, chiming in the breeze that came through the open windows.

The lieutenant governor was just ascending to his place. He dropped his gavel to the sounding board of his desk.

"The Senate will be in order," he said.

The chaplain rose and the hum of voices in the chamber ceased. Then, while the senators stood with bowed heads, Morley saw the card that lay on the desk beside the rose. Two little jewels of the moisture that still sparkled on the rose's petals shone on the glazed surface of the card. Morley read it where it lay.

"Will the Hon. Morley Vernon please wear this rose today as a token of his intention to support and vote for House Joint Resolution No. 19, proposing an amendment to Section 1, Article VII, of the Constitution?"

The noise in the chamber began again at the chaplain's "Amen."

"New way to buttonhole a man, eh?" said Morley to Bull Burns, who occupied the next seat. "What's it all about, anyway?"

Morley took up his printed synopsis of bills and resolutions.

"Oh, yes," he said, speaking as much to himself as to Burns, "old man Ames's resolution." Then he turned to the calendar. There it was—House Joint Resolution No. 19. He glanced at Burns again. Burns was fastening his rose in his buttonhole.

"So you're for it, eh?" he asked.

Burns grumbled a denial that spoke for the First District. In trying to look down at his own adornment he screwed his fat neck, fold on fold, into his low collar and then, with a grunt of satisfaction, lit a morning cigar.

"But—" Morley began, surprises multiplying. He looked about the chamber. The secretary was reading the journal of the preceding day and the senators were variously occupied, reading newspapers, writing letters, or merely smoking. Some were gathered in little groups, talking and laughing. But they all wore their roses. Morley might have concluded that House Joint Resolution No. 19 was safe, had it not been for the inconsistency of Burns, though inconsistency was nothing new in

21

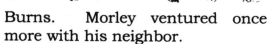

Burns.   Morley   ventured   once
more with his neighbor.

"Looks as if the resolution were
as good as adopted, doesn't it?"

But burns cast a glance of pity
at him, and then growled in half-
humorous contempt. The action
stung Morley. Burns seemed to
resent his presence in the Senate
as he always resented the presence of Morley's kind in politics.

The rose still lay on Morley's
desk. He was the only one of the
fifty-one senators of Illinois that
had not put his rose on. He
opened his bill file and turned up
House Joint Resolution No. 19.
He read it carefully, as he felt a
senator should before making up
his mind on such an important,
even revolutionary measure. He
remembered that at the time it
had been adopted in the House,
everyone had laughed. No one,

22

with the exception of its author, Dr. Ames, had taken it seriously.

Ames was known to be a crank. He was referred to as "Doc" Ames, usually as "Old Doc" Ames. He had introduced more strange bills and resolutions than any member at that session—bills to curb the homeopathists, bills to annihilate English sparrows, bills to prohibit cigarettes, bills to curtail the liquor traffic, and now this resolution providing for the submission of an amendment to the Constitution that would extend the electoral franchise to women.

His other measures had received little consideration. He never got any of them out of committee. But on the female suffrage resolution he had been obdurate, and when—with a majority so bare that sick men had to be borne on cots into the House now and then

23

to pass its measures—the party had succeeded, after weeks of agony in framing an apportionment bill that satisfied everyone, Dr. Ames had seen his chance. He had flatly refused to vote for the reapportionment act unless his woman-suffrage resolution were first adopted.

It was useless for the party managers to urge upon him the impossibility of providing the necessary two-thirds' vote. Ames said he could get the remaining votes from the other side. And so the steering committee had given the word to put it through for him. Then the other side, seeing a chance to place the majority in an embarrassing attitude before the people, either as the proponents or the opponents of such a radical measure—whichever way it went in the end—had been glad enough to furnish the additional votes. The members of the steering committee had afterward whispered it about that the resolution was to die in the Senate. Then everyone, especially the women of Illinois, had promptly forgotten the measure.

As Morley thought over it all he picked up the rose again, then laid it down, and idly picked up the card. Turning it over in his hand he saw that its other side was engraved, and he read:

MARIA BURLEY GREENE
ATTORNEY AND COUNSELOR AT LAW

THE ROOKERY   CHICAGO

Then he knew. It was the work of the woman lawyer. Morley had heard of her often. He had never seen her. He gave a little sniff of disgust.

The Senate was droning along on the order of reports from standing committees, and Morley, growing tired of the monotony, rose and sauntered back to the lobby in search of company more congenial than that of gruff Burns. He carried the rose as he went, raising it now and then to enjoy its cool petals and its fragrance. On one of the leather divans that stretch themselves invitingly under the tall windows on each side of the Senate chamber sat a woman, and about her was a little group of men, bending deferentially. As he passed within easy distance one of the men saw him and beckoned.   Morley went over to them.

"Miss Greene," said Senator Martin, "let me present Senator Vernon, of Chicago."

Miss Greene gave him the little hand that looked yet smaller in its glove of black suede.   He bowed low to conceal a surprise that had sprung incautiously to his eyes. Instead of the thin, shorthaired, spectacled old maid that had always, in his mind, typified Maria Burley Greene, here was a young woman who apparently conformed to every fashion, though her beauty and distinction might have made her independent of conventions.   Physically she was too nearly perfect to give at once an impression of aristocracy; but it was her expression that charmed; it was plain that her intellectuality was of the higher degrees.

27

As Morley possessed himself he was able to note that this surprising young woman was clad in a black traveling gown that fitted her perfectly. From her spring had down to the toes of her boots there was nothing in her attire that was mannish, but she was of an exquisite daintiness wholly feminine and alluring.

All these superficial things faded into their proper background when, at last, his eyes looked full in her face. Reddish brown hair that doubtless had been combed into some resemblance to the prevailing fashion of the pompadour had fallen in a natural part on the right side and lightly swept a brow not too high, but white and thoughtful. Her other features—the delicate nose, the full lips, the perfect teeth, the fine chin—all were lost in the eyes

28

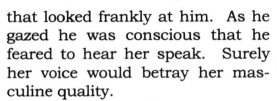

that looked frankly at him. As he gazed he was conscious that he feared to hear her speak. Surely her voice would betray her masculine quality.

She had seated herself again, and now made a movement that suggested a drawing aside of her skirts to make a place for someone at her side. And then she spoke.

"Will you sit down, Senator Vernon?" she invited, with a scrupulous regard for title unusual in a woman. "I must make a convert of Senator Vernon, you know," she smiled on the other men about her. Her accent implied that this conversion was of the utmost importance. The other men, of whom she seemed to be quite sure, evidently felt themselves under the compulsion of withdrawing, and so fell back in reluctant retreat.

III

THE surprise had leaped to Morley's eyes again at the final impression of perfection made by her voice, and the surprise changed to a regret of lost and irreclaimable opportunity when he reflected that he had lived for years near this woman lawyer and yet never had seen her once in all that time. When Miss Greene turned to look him in the face again, after the others were gone, Morley grew suddenly bashful, like a big boy. He felt his face flame hotly. He had been meditating some drawing-room speech; he had already turned in his mind a pretty sentence in which there was a discreet reference to Portia. Morley was just at the age for classical allusions. But when he saw her blue eyes fixed on him and read the utter seriousness in them he knew that compliments would all be lost.

"I am one of your constituents, Senator Vernon," she began, "and I am down, frankly, lobbying for this resolution."

"And we both," he replied, "are, I believe, members of the Cook County bar. Strange, isn't it, that two Chicago lawyers should have to wait until they are in Springfield to meet?"

"Not altogether," she said. "It is not so very strange—my practice is almost wholly confined to office work. I am more of a counselor than a barrister. I have not often

31

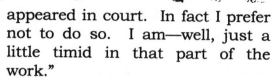

appeared in court. In fact I prefer not to do so. I am—well, just a little timid in that part of the work."

The femininity of it touched him. He might have told her that he did not often appear in court himself, but he was new enough at the bar to have to practice the dissimulation of the young professional man. He indulged himself in the temptation to allow her to go undeceived, though with a pang he remembered that her practice, from all that he had heard, must be much more lucrative than his. Something of the pretty embarrassment she felt before courts and juries was evidently on her in this her first appearance in the Senate, but she put it away. Her breast rose with the deep breath of resolution she drew, and she straightened to look him once more in the eyes.

"But about this resolution, Senator Vernon, I must not take up too much of your time. If you will give me your objections to it perhaps I may be able to explain them away. We should very much like to have your support."

Morley scarcely knew what to reply. Such objections as he might have found at other times— the old masculine objections to women's voting and meddling in politics—had all disappeared at sight of this remarkable young woman who wished to vote herself. He could not think of one of them, try as he would. His eyes were on the rose.

"Perhaps your objections are merely prejudices," she ventured boldly, in her eyes a latent twinkle that disturbed him.

"I confess, Miss Greene," he began, trying to get back something of his senatorial dignity, such as state senatorial dignity is, "that I have not devoted much thought to the subject. I am indeed rather ashamed to acknowledge that I did not even know the amendment was coming up today, until I was—ah—so delightfully reminded by your rose."

He raised the rose to inhale its fragrance. She made no reply, but she kept her eyes on him, and her gaze compelled him to go on. It was hard for him to go on, for it was now but a struggle against the formality of a surrender that had been inevitable from the beginning. But this man's pride forced him to delay it as long as possible.

"What assurances have you from other senators?" he asked. "Though, perhaps, I need not

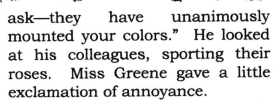

ask—they have unanimously mounted your colors." He looked at his colleagues, sporting their roses. Miss Greene gave a little exclamation of annoyance.

"Do you think I don't know," she said, "that I don't understand all that? I might have known that they would not take it seriously! And I thought—I thought—to put the matter so easily to them that I should be spared the necessity of buttonholing them!"

"It was a novel way of button-holing them," he laughed.

"Oh!" she exclaimed, catching her breath, "they wear the roses—and laugh at me!"

Her eyes flashed through the mists of vexation that suggested tears.

"You are all alone then?"

Morley said this in a low, solicitous tone, as if he were dealing with some deep grief.

"All alone."

"And you represent no one— that is, no society, no club?"

"I am not a paid lobbyist," she said, "though I believe it is not beyond the proprieties of our profession. I do what I do only from a love of principle. I represent only my sex." She said it impressively, and then with a quick little laugh that recognized the theatrical that had been in her attitude, she added, "And that, I suspect, without authorization."

"The ladies, generally, do not seem to be interested," Morley acquiesced.

"No," she shook her head sadly, "No, on the contrary, I suppose most of them oppose the measure."

"I have generally found them of that feeling," Morley observed.

"The slaves, before the war, often petitioned congress not to set them free, you will remember."

Miss Greene spoke with a bitterness. Then quickly she collected herself.

"But your objections, Senator Vernon?" she asked again. "Really, we must get down to business."

She raised the little chatelaine watch that hung at her bosom and looked down at it. And then suddenly, without waiting for his objections, as if she had quite forgotten them indeed, she impulsively stretched forth a hand and said, "You will help me, won't you?"

Morley looked into her eyes. His gaze, after an instant, fell. He tried to run the stem of the rose

37

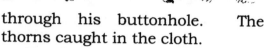

through his buttonhole. The thorns caught in the cloth.

"You'll have to do it," he said, helplessly.

From some mysterious fold of her habit she took a pin, and then, leaning over, she pinned the rose to his coat, pinned it with its long stem hanging, as a woman would pin a flower to a man's lapel.

"Thank you." He was looking into her eyes again.

"Rather let me thank *you*," she said. "It's so good of you to vote for my measure."

His eyes widened suddenly. He had quite forgotten the resolution. She must have perceived this, for she blushed, and he hastened to make amends.

"I'll not only vote for it," he rushed ahead impulsively, "but I'll make a speech for it." He straightened and leaned away from her to give a proper perspective in which she could admire him. He sat there smiling.

"How splendid of you!" she cried. "I feel encouraged now."

Then Morley's face lengthened. He stammered. "But you'll have to give me some data. I—I don't know a thing about the subject."

"Oh," she laughed, "I brought some literature. It shall all be at your disposal. And now, I must be about my work. Can you make any suggestions? Can you tell me whom I should see, whom I should interest, who had the—ah—pull, I believe you call it?"

"I'll bring them to you," Morley said. "You sit here and hold court."

He rose and his eyes swept the chamber. They lighted on Burns, and an idea suddenly came to him. He would revenge himself on

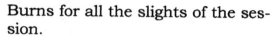

Burns for all the slights of the session.

"Of course you'll have to see
Sam Porter, but I'll begin by
bringing Senator Burns—familiarly known as Bull Burns."

"I've read of him so often in the
newspapers," she said. "It would
be an experience."

Morley went over to Burns's
seat and touched him on the
shoulder.

"Come on," he said in a tone of
command, speaking for once from
the altitude of his social superiority. And for once he was successful. The burly fellow from the
First District stood up and looked
inquiringly.

"Come with me," Morley said.
"There's a Chicago lawyer back
here who wants to see you."

Burns followed and an instant
later Morley halted before Miss

Greene. The other men, who had quickly returned to her side, made way, and Vernon said, "Miss Greene, may I present Senator Burns, of the First District?"

Miss Greene smiled on the big saloonkeeper, who instantly flamed with embarrassment. She gave him her hand, and he took it in his fat palm, carefully, lest he crush it.

"I am delighted to meet Senator Burns. I've heard of you so often," she said, looking up at him. "And do you know I count it a privilege to meet one of your acknowledged influence in our state's affairs?"

Morley stood back, delighted beyond measure with the confusion into which Burns for once had been betrayed. The senator from the First District was struggling for some word to say, and at last he replied.

41

"Aw now, lady, don't be t'rowin' de con into me."

The men in the little group on that side of the Senate chamber burst out in a laugh, but Burns becoming suddenly grave, and dangerous and terrible in his gravity, they broke off in the very midst of their mirth. The group became silent.

"Really, Senator Burns," said Miss Greene, "this is no—ah—confidence game, I assure you." She rose with a graceful sweep of her skirts. Then she went on. "If you will permit me, I should like to explain my mission to you. I am down here to ask the Senate to adopt a resolution that will submit an amendment to the Constitution permitting the women of Illinois to vote at all elections, as they vote at school elections now. If you can give it, I should like your support.

42

I should, at least, like to tell you my reasons."

Slowly she seated herself again, saying, "Will you sit down?"

But Burns only stood and looked at her. There was a trace of fear in her face.

"Do *you* want dis resolution put t'rough?" he asked bluntly.

"I? Indeed I do!" she said.

"Is dere anyt'ing in it fer you?" he went on.

"Why," Miss Green said, somewhat at a loss, "only that I am interested as a matter of principle in seeing it adopted. It would be a great day for me if I could go back to Chicago feeling that I had had just a little bit to do with such a result."

"Den I'm wit' you," said Burns, and wheeling, he went back to his desk.

Miss Greene watched him a moment, and then turned to the men, their numbers augmented now by others who had come up to see Burns in the presence of such a woman. The glance she gave them was a question.

"Oh, he means it," said Monroe of Whiteside. "He'll vote for the resolution."

"Yes, he's given his word," said Brownell of Cook.

Morley devoted half an hour to bringing senators to meet Maria Greene. It was not difficult work, though it had its disadvantages. It did not allow Morley to remain with her long at a time. But at last it was done, and he found a moment alone with her. She had given him some pamphlets on equal suffrage.

"Ah, if *you* could only address the Senate!" he exclaimed, in open

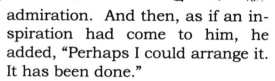

admiration. And then, as if an in-
spiration had come to him, he
added, "Perhaps I could arrange it.
It has been done."

She gasped and stretched out
her hand to stay him.

"Oh, not for all the world!" she
protested.

"But you'll come and meet the
lieutenant governor?"

"Up there?" she asked, pointing
to the dais under the flags.

"Why, yes," Morley answered.
"Why not? It's where all the eminent lawyers sit who come down
here to lobby."

She looked up at the desk behind which the lieutenant governor sat, swinging gently in his
swivel chair, while the secretary
read Senate bills on third reading.
There was a reluctance in her
eyes, but when she caught

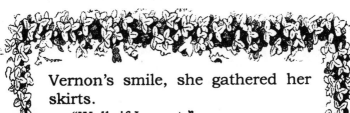

Vernon's smile, she gathered her skirts.

"Well, if I must."

IV

WHILE Miss Greene sat chatting with the lieutenant governor, who gladly neglected the duties of his high office, Morley went out into the rotunda, pulled a toothpick from his pocket to chew on, and tried to arrange the heads of his speech in his mind.

At the thought of the speech, Morley grew cold and limp with nervousness. His hands were clammy, his knees trembled, his mouth became dry and parched, and the toothpick he had chewed to a pulp imparted all at once an evil taste. Yet he chewed on, and as he wandered around the rotunda, men from both houses, passing to and fro, greeted him, but they seemed to him to be strange new creatures flitting by in a dream. If he was conscious of them at all it was only as of envied beings, all on a common happy plane, fortunate ones who did not have to make a speech within the hour. He went over to the state library, thinking that its quiet would soothe, but when he stood among the tall stacks of books he suddenly remembered that he must not talk in those precincts and so he turned out into the rotunda again to practice aloud the words he would deliver. He walked round and round the rotunda, pausing at times to lean over the brass railing and look far down to the main floor where the red light glowed at the cigar stand. He sauntered back into the dim and undisturbed corridors, his mind racing ahead of the words he was mumbling.

Once or twice he glanced into the pamphlets Miss Greene had given him, but he could not fix his mind on them. Their types danced meaninglessly before his eyes. He was angry with himself for this nervousness. Why must it assail him now, just when he wished to be at his best? He had spoken before, a hundred times. He knew his audience, and he had the proper contempt for his colleagues. He had never, to be sure, made a set speech in that presence. Seldom did anyone do that. The speeches were usually short and impromptu, and there was no time for anticipation to generate nervous dread. And yet his mind seemed to be extraordinarily clear just then. It seemed to be able to comprehend all realms of thought at once.

But it was not so much the speech he thought of, as the effect of the speech. Already he could see the newspapers and the big headlines they would display on their first pages the next morning. He could see his mother reading them at breakfast, and then he could see Amelia reading them. How her dark eyes would widen, her cheeks flush pink! She would raise her hand and put back her hair with that pretty mannerism of hers. Then impulsively resting her arms on the table before her, she would eagerly read the long columns through, while her mother reminded her that her breakfast was getting cold. How proud she would be of him! She would never chide him again. She would see that at last he had found himself.

51

The Eltons, too, would read, and his absence from their dinner would react on them impressively. And Maria Greene—but a confusion arose—Maria Greene! He had not thought of Amelia all the morning until that very instant. Amelia's letter lay still unopened on his desk back there in the Senate chamber. Maria Greene! She would hear, she would color as she looked at him, and her eyes would glow. He could feel the warm pressure of the hand she would give him in congratulation.

And it was this handsome young woman's presence in the chamber that gave rise to all this nervousness. He was sure that he would not have been nervous if Amelia were to be there. She had never heard him speak in public, though he had often pressed her to hear him. Somehow the places where he spoke were never those to which it would be proper for her to go. She would wish she had heard this speech, for in twenty-four hours it would be the one topic of conversation throughout the state. His picture would be in the newspapers—"The brilliant young Chicago lawyer who electrified the Illinois Senate with his passionate oratory and passed the woman-suffrage measure." It would be an event to mark the beginning of a new era—

But his imaginings were broken, his name was spoken. He turned and saw Miss Greene.

"Come," she said. "It's up! Hurry!"

She was excited and her cheeks glowed. His teeth began to chatter. He followed her quick steps in the direction of the chamber.

"But," he stammered. "I—I didn't know—I haven't even arranged for recognition."

"Oh, I've fixed all that!" the woman said. "The lieutenant governor promised me." She was holding her rustling skirts and almost running.

V

AS they entered the Senate chamber, Morley heard the lieutenant governor say, "And the question is: Shall the resolution be adopted? Those in favor will vote 'aye,' those opposed will vote 'no,' when their names are called. And the secretary will call the—"

"Mr. President!" Morley shouted. There was no time now to retreat. He had launched himself on the sea of glory. A dozen other senators were on their feet, likewise demanding recognition.

"The senator from Cook," said the lieutenant governor.

Morley stood by his desk, arranging complacently the documents Miss Greene had given him. Once or twice he cleared his throat and wiped his lips with his handkerchief. The other senators subsided into their seats, and, seeing that they themselves were not then to be permitted to speak, and like all speakers, not caring to listen to the speeches of others, they turned philosophically to the little diversions with which they whiled away the hours of the session—writing letters, reading newspapers, smoking. Morley glanced around. Maria Greene was sitting precariously on the edge of a divan. Her face was white and drawn. She gave a quick nod, and a smile just touched her fixed lips. And then Morley began. He spoke slowly and with vast deliberation. His voice was very low. He outlined his subject with exquisite pains, detail by detail, making it clear just what propositions he would advance. His manner was that of the lawyer in an appellate court, making a masterly and purely legal argument. When it was done, the Senate, if it had paid attention—would know all about the question of woman-suffrage.

In his deliberation, Morley glanced now and then at Maria Greene. Her eyes were sparkling with intelligent interest. As if to choose the lowest point possible from which to trace the rise and progress of legislation favorable to women, Morley would call the attention of the Senate, first, to the decision of the Illinois Supreme Court *In re* Bradwell, 55 Ill. 525. That was away back in 1869, when the age was virtually dark. And that was the case, gentlemen

would remember, just as if they all
kept each decision of the court at
their tongues' ends, in which the
court held that no woman could
be admitted, under the laws of Illinois, to practice as an attorney at
law. But—and Morley implored
his colleagues to mark—long years
afterward, the court of its own
motion, entered a *nunc pro tunc*
order, reversing its own decision
in the Bradwell case. Morley di-
lated upon the importance of this
decision. He extolled the court. It
had set a white milestone to mark
the progressing emancipation of
the race. Then, briefly, he pro-
posed to outline for them the legislative steps by which woman's
right to equality with man had
been at least partly recognized.

He fumbled for a moment
among the papers on his desk,
until he found one of the pam-

phlets Miss Greene had given him, and then he said he wished to call the Senate's attention to the Employment Act of 1872, the Drainage Act of 1885, and the Sanitary District Act of 1890. Morley spoke quite familiarly of these acts. Furthermore, gentlemen would, he was sure, instantly recall the decisions of the courts in which those acts were under review, as for instance, in Wilson *vs.* Board of Trustees, 133 Ill. 443; and in Davenport *vs.* Drainage Commissioners, 25 Ill. App. 92.

Those among the senators who were lawyers, as most of them were, looked up from their letter writing at this, and nodded profoundly, in order to show their familiarity with Morley's citations, although, of course, they never had heard of the cases before.

"This recognition of woman's natural right," Morley shouted, "this recognition of her equality with man, can not be overestimated in importance!" He shook his head fiercely and struck his desk with his fist. But then, having used up all the facts he had marked in Miss Greene's pamphlets, he was forced to become more general in his remarks, and so he began to celebrate woman, ecstatically. He conjured for the senators the presence of their mothers and sisters, their sweethearts and wives. And then, some quotations fortunately occurring to him, he reminded them that Castiglione had truly said that "God is seen only through women," that "the woman's soul leadeth us upward and on." He recounted the services of women in time of war, their deeds in the

60

days of peace, and in the end he
became involved in an allegory
about the exclusion of the roses
from the garden.

The Senators had begun to pay
attention to him as soon as he
talked about things they really
understood and were interested in,
and now they shouted to him to go
on. It was spread abroad over the
third floor of the State House that
someone was making a speech in
the Senate, and representatives
came rushing over from the
House. The correspondents of the
Chicago newspapers came over
also to see if the Associated Press
man in the Senate was getting the
speech down fully. All the space
on the Senate floor was soon
crowded, and the applause shook
the desks and made the glass
prisms on the chandeliers jingle.
The lieutenant governor tapped

from time to time with his gavel, but he did it perfunctorily, as though he enjoyed the applause himself, as vicariously expressing his own feelings. His eyes twinkled until it seemed that, were it not for certain traditions, he would join in the delighted laughter that made up most of the applause.

Once a page came to Morley with a glass of water, and he paused to wipe his brow and to sip from the glass, he glanced again at Maria Greene. Her face was solemn and a wonder was growing in her eyes. Beside her sat old Doc Ames, scowling fiercely and stroking his long white beard. There were sharp cries of "Go on! Go on!"

But Morley, not accustomed to thinking on his feet, as talkers love to phrase it, and having stopped, could not instantly go on,

and that awkward halt discon-
certed him. He was conscious that
the moments were slipping by,
and there were other things—
many other things—which he had
intended to say. But these things
evaded him—floated off, tantaliz-
ingly, out of reach. And so, for
refuge, he rushed on to the conclusion he had half formed in his
mind. The conclusion was made
up mostly from a toast to which he
had once responded while in college, entitled, "The Ladies." The
words came back to him readily
enough. He had only to apply
them a little differently and to
change his figures. Thus it was
easy to work up to a panegyric in
which Illinois stood as a beautiful
woman leading her sister states
up to new heights of peace, of
virtue and of concord. He had a
rapt vision of this woman, by her

sweet and gentle influence settling all disputes and bringing heaven down to earth at last.

The Senate was in raptures.

"This is the face, he cried, "'that launched a thousand ships and burned the topless towers of Iliu!' . . . 'she is wholly like in feature to the deathless goddesses!'" So he went on. "'Age can not wither, nor custom stale, her infinite variety.'"

He was growing weary. He already showed the impressive exhaustion of the peroration. He had sacrificed a collar and drunk all the water from his glass. He fingered the empty tumbler for a moment, and then lifted it on high while he said:

"'I filled this cup to one made up
Of loveliness alone,
A woman, of her gentle sex
The seeming paragon—
Her health! And would on earth

65

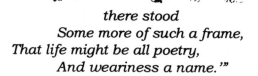

there stood
Some more of such a frame,
That life might be all poetry,
And weariness a name.'"

When he had done, there was a moment's stillness. Then came the long sweep of applause that rang through the chamber, and while the lieutenant governor rapped for order, men crowded around Morley and wrung his hand, as he wiped his forehead with his handkerchief. And then the roll was called. It had not proceeded far when there was that subtle change n the atmosphere which is so easily recognized by those who have acquired the sense of political aeroscepsy—the change that betokens some new, unexpected and dangerous maneuver. Braidwood had come over from the House. His face, framed in its dark beard, was stern and serious.

He whispered an instant to Porter, the Senate leader. Porter rose.

"Mr. President," he said.

The lieutenant governor was looking at him expectantly.

"The gentleman from Cook," the lieutenant governor said.

"Mr. President," said Senator Porter, "I move you, sir, that the further discussion of the resolution be postponed until Wednesday morning, one week from tomorrow, and that it be made a special order immediately following the reading of the journal."

"If there are no objections it will be so ordered," said the lieutenant governor.

Bull Burns shouted a prompt and hoarse, "Object!"

But the lieutenant governor calmly said, "And it is so ordered."

The gavel fell.

VI

AFTER the adjournment Morley sought out Maria Greene and walked with her down Capitol Avenue toward the hotel. He was prepared to enjoy her congratulations, but she was silent for a while, and before they spoke again Doc Ames, striding rapidly, had caught up with them. He was still scowling.

"I was sorry you didn't finish your speech as you intended, sir," he said, with something of the acerbity of a reproach.

"Why," began Morley, looking at him, "I—"

"You laid out very broad and comprehensive ground for your-

68

self," the old man continued, "but unfortunately you did not cover it. You should have developed your subject logically, as I had hopes, indeed, in the beginning, you were going to do. An argument based on principle would have been more to the point than an appeal to the passions. I think Miss Greene will agree with me. I am sorry you did not acquaint me with your intention of addressing the Senate on this important measure; I would very much have liked to confer with you about what you were going to say. It is not contemplated by those in the reform movement that the charms of woman shall be advanced as the reason for her right to equal suffrage with man. It is purely a matter of cold, abstract justice. Now, for instance," the doctor laid his finger in his palm, and began to speak didactically, "as I have pointed out to the House, whatever the power or the principle that gives to man his right to make the law that governs him, to woman it gives the same right. In thirty-seven states the married mother has no right to her children; in sixteen the wife has no right to her own earnings; in eight she has no separate right to her property; in seven—"

Morley looked at Miss Greene helplessly, but she was nodding her head in acquiescence to each point the doctor laid down in his harsh palm with that long forefinger. Morley had no chance to speak until they reached the hotel. She was to take the midday train back to Chicago, and Morley had insisted on going to the station with her.

Just as she was about to leave him to go up to her room she said, as on a sudden impulse, "Do you know that the women of America, yes, the people of America, owe you a debt?"

Morley assumed a most modest attitude.

"If we are successful," she went on, "the advocates of equal suffrage all over the United States will be greatly encouraged. The reform movement everywhere will receive a genuine impetus."

"You will be down next Wednesday when the resolution comes up again, won't you?" asked Morley.

"Indeed, I shall," she said. "Do you have any hopes now?"

"Hopes?" laughed Morley. "Why certainly. We'll adopt it. I'll give my whole time to it between now and then. If they don't adopt

71

that resolution I'll block every other piece of legislation this session, appropriations and all. I guess that will bring them to time!"

"You're very good," she said. "But I fear Mr. Porter's influence."

"Oh, I'll take care of him. You trust it to me. The women will be voting in this state next year."

"And you shall be their candidate for governor!" she cried, clasping her hands.

Morley colored. He felt a warm thrill course through him, but he waved the nomination aside with his hand. He was about to say something more, but he could not think of anything quickly enough. While he hesitated, Miss Greene looked at her watch.

"I've missed my train," she said, quietly.

Morley grew red with confusion.

"I beg a thousand pardons!" he said "It was all my fault and it was certainly very stupid of me."

"It's of no importance. Where must I go to reserve space on the night train?" she asked.

Morley told her, and proffered his services. He was now delighted at the philosophical way in which she accepted the situation—it would have brought the average woman, he reflected, to tears—and then he went onto picture to himself the practical results in improving women's characters that his new measure, as he had already come to regard it, would bring about.

VII

MARIA GREENE would not
let Morley attend to her
tickets. She said it was a
matter of principle with her. But
late in the afternoon, when they
had had luncheon, and she had
got the tickets herself, she did accept his invitation to drive. The
afternoon had justified all the
morning's promise of a fine spring
day, and as they left the edges of
the town and turned into the road
that stretched away over the low
undulations of ground they call
hills in Illinois, and lost itself
mysteriously in the country far
beyond, Miss Greene became en-
thusiastic.

"Isn't it glorious!" she cried. "And to think that when I left Chicago last night it was still winter!" She shuddered, as if she would shake off the memory of the city's ugliness. Her face was flushed and she inhaled the sweet air eagerly.

"To be in the country once more!" she went on.

"Did you ever live in the country?" Morley asked.

"Once," she said, and then after a grave pause she added, "a long time ago."

The road they had turned into was as soft and as smooth as velvet now that the spring had released it from the thrall of winter's mud. It led beside a golf links, and the new greens were already dotted with golfers, who played with the zest they had accumulated in the forbidding winter

75

months. They showed their en-
thusiasm by playing bare-armed,
as if already it were the height of
summer.

As the buggy rolled noiselessly
along, Morley and Miss Greene
were silent. The spell of the spring
was on them. To their right rolled
the prairies, that never can become mere fields, however much
they be tilled or fenced. The
brown earth, with its tinge of
young green here and there, or its
newly ploughed clods glistening
and steaming in the sun, rolled
away like the sea. Far off, standing out black and forbidding
against the horizon, they could see
the ugly buildings of a coal shaft.
Behind, above the trees that grew
for the city's shade, the convent
lifted its tower, and above all, the
gray dome of the State House
reared itself, dominating the whole

scene. The air shimmered in the haze of spring. Birds were chirping in the hedges. Now and then a meadowlark sprang into the air and fled, crying out its strange staccato song as it skimmed the surface of the prairies. Neither Morley nor Maria seemed to care to speak. Suddenly they heard a distant, heavy thud. The earth trembled slightly.

"What's that?" asked Miss Greene with alarm. "It couldn't have been thunder."

"No," said Morley, "it was the miners, blasting."

"Where?"

"Down in the ground underneath us."

She gave him a strange look, which he did not comprehend. Then she turned and glanced quickly at the black breakers of

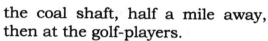

the coal shaft, half a mile away, then at the golf-players.

"Do the mines run under this ground?" she asked sweeping her hand about and including the links in her gesture.

"Yes, all over here, or rather under here," Morley said. He was proud of his knowledge of the locality. He thought it argued well that a legislator should be informed on all questions.

Maria thought a moment, then said, "The golfers above, the miners below."

Morley looked at her in surprise. The pleasure of the spring had gone out of her eyes.

"Drive on, please," she said.

"There's no danger," said Morley reassuringly, clucking at his horse. The beast flung up its head in a spasmodic burst of speed, as livery-stable horses will. The

horse did not have to trot very far
to bear them away from the crack
of the golf balls and the dull sub-
terranean echoes of the miners'
blasts, but Morley felt that a cloud
had floated all at once over this
first spring day. The woman sitting there beside him seemed to
withdraw herself to an infinite
distance.

"You love the country?" he
asked, feeling the need of speech.

"Yes," she replied, but she went
no further.

"And you once lived there?"

"Yes," she said again, but she
vouchsafed no more. Morley
found a deep curiosity springing
within him. He longed to know
more about this young woman
who in all outward ways seemed to
be just like the women he knew,
and yet was so essentially different
from them. But though he tried,

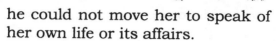

he could not move her to speak of her own life or its affairs.

At last he said boldly, "Tell me, how did you come to be a lawyer?"

Miss Greene turned to meet his inquisitive gaze.

"How did you?" she asked.

Morley cracked his whip at the road.

"Well—" he stammered. "I don't know. I had to do something."

"So did I," she replied.

Morley cracked the whip above the horse's ears and the buggy jerked as the creature made its professional feint at trotting.

"I did not care to lead a useless life," he said. "I wanted to do something—to have some part in the world's work. The law seemed to be a respectable profession and I felt that maybe I could do some good in politics. I don't think the men of my class take as much interest in politics as they should. And then, I'd like to make my own living."

"I have to make mine," said Maria Greene.

"But you never thought of teaching, or nursing, or—well—painting or music, or that sort of thing, did you?"

"No, she replied, "did you?"

Morley laughed at an absurdity that needed no answering comment, and then he hastened on.

"Of course, you know I think it fine that you should have done as you have. You must have met with discouragements."

She laughed, and Morley did not note the bitterness there was concealed in the laugh. To him it seemed intended to express only that polite deprecation demanded

81

in the treatment of a personal situation.

"I can sympathize with you there," said Vernon, though Miss Greene had not admitted the need of sympathy. Perhaps it was Morley's own need of sympathy, or his feeling of the need of it, that made him confess that his own family and friends had never sympathized with him, especially with what he called his work in politics. He felt, at any rate, that he had struck the right note at last, and he went on to assure her how unusual it was to meet a woman who understood public questions as well as she understood them. And it may have been his curiosity that led him to his next inquiry.

"How did your people feel about your taking up the law?"

Miss Greene said that she did not know how her people felt, and

Morley again had that baffled sense of her evading him.

"I've felt pretty much alone in my work," he said. "The women I know won't talk with me about it. They won't even read the newspapers. And I've tried so hard to interest them in it!"

Morley sighed, and he waited for Miss Greene to sigh with him. He did not look at her, but he could feel her presence there close beside him. Her gloved hands lay quietly in her lap. She was gazing out over the prairies. The light winds were faintly stirring her hair, and the beauty of it, its warm red tones brought out by the burnishing sun, suddenly overwhelmed him. He stirred and his breath came hard.

"Do you know," he said, in a new confidence, "that this has been a great day for me? To meet

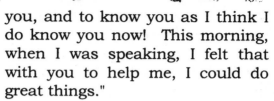

you, and to know you as I think I do know you now! This morning, when I was speaking, I felt that with you to help me, I could do great things."

Miss Greene drew in her lips, as if to compress their fullness. She moved away on the seat, and raised her hand uneasily and thrust it under her veil to put back a tress of hair that had strayed from its fastening. Morley saw the flush of her white cheeks come and go. Her eyebrows were drawn together wistfully, and in her blue eyes that looked far away through the meshes of her dotted veil, there was a little cloud of trouble. She caught her lip delicately between the edges of her teeth.

Morley leaned slightly forward as if he would peer into her face. For him the day had grown suddenly hot, the spring had developed on the instant the oppressive heat of summer. He felt its fire. He could see its intensity vibrating in the air all about him, and he had a sense as of all the summer's voices droning in unison. The reins drooped from his listless fingers. The horse moped along as it pleased.

"I have always felt that I have stood on the fringe of real success," Morley went on, his voice dropping to a low tone, "but this morning—"

Miss Greene raised her hand as if to draw it across her brow. Her veil stopped her.

"Let's not talk about that now," she pleaded. "Let's enjoy the air and the country. I don't have them often." Her hand fell to her lap. The color had gone out of her cheeks. And Morley suddenly felt that the summer had gone out of the air. A cold wind was blowing as over soiled patches of snow left in shaded depressions of the fields. The earth was brown and bare. The birds were silent. He jerked the reins and the horse gave an angry toss of its head as it broke into its tentative trot.

"I do wish you could know the women I know," said Morley, obviously breaking a silence. He spoke in an entirely different voice. "I meant to put it the other way. I meant that I wish they could know you, and I mean that they shall. You would be a revelation to them."

Miss Greene smiled, though her face was now careworn, almost old.

"Right along the line of our constitutional amendment, now," he said, with a briskness, "do you

86

think the women will become interested?"

"The women of your acquaintance, or of mine?" asked Miss Greene.

"You're guying," said Morley, and when Miss Greene seriously protested, Morley said he meant all the women, as politicians pretend to mean all the people, when they mean only the party.

"I'm afraid not," she said. "They could have the ballot tomorrow if they'd only ask for it. The trouble is they don't want it."

"Well, we must educate them," said Morley. "I have great hopes that the women whom I know will be aroused by what we are doing."

"I have no doubt they will," said Miss Greene. There was something enigmatic in her words, and Morley glanced uneasily at her again.

87

"How do you mean?" he asked.

"You'll learn when you see the newspapers tomorrow," said Miss Greene.

"Do you think they'll have it in full?" asked Morley. He was all alert, and his eyes sparkled in a new interest.

"On the first page," she replied with conviction. "Have they your picture?"

"I don't know," Morley replied. "They can get it, though," he added thoughtfully.

"They keep the portraits of all distinguished public men on hand," Miss Greene said, with a certain reassurance in her tone.

"Oh, well, I hope they'll not print it," said Morley, as if just then recalling what was expected of a distinguished public man under such circumstances.

"That's one of the penalties of being in public life," she answered with a curious smile.

"A penalty the ladies will be glad to pay when our reform is accomplished. Isn't that so?" asked Morley, seeking relief in a light bantering tone.

"I thought we were not going to talk politics," she said, turning and looking at him. She adjusted her hat and held herself resolutely erect.

The sun was going down behind the prairies, the afternoon was almost gone. As they watched the sunset, Miss Greene broke the silence.

"It's a familiar sight," she said, and Morley thought that he had a clue at last. She must know the prairies.

"It is just like a sunset at sea," she added.

90

When they had driven back to the town and Morley had left her at the hotel, he turned to drive to the livery stable.

"By George!" he said suddenly to himself. "I haven't read Amelia's letter!"

He fumbled in his coat pocket.

VIII

MISS GREENE'S predictions were all realized in the sensation Morley's speech created. The newspapers gave whole columns to it and illustrated their accounts with portraits of Morley and of Maria Greene. Morley thought of the pleasure Amelia must find in his new fame, and when he wrote to her he referred briefly but with the proper modesty to his remarkable personal triumph, and then waited for her congratulations.

The legislative session was drawing to a close. The customary Friday adjournment was not taken, but sessions were held that day and on Saturday, for the work was piling up, the procrastinating legislators having left it all for the last minute.

The week following would see House and Senate sweltering in shirt sleeves and night sessions, and now, if a bill were to become law it was necessary that its sponsor stay, as it were, close beside it, lest in the mighty rush of the last few days it be lost.

Morley, by virtue of his speech, had assumed the championship of the woman-suffrage resolution, and he felt it necessary to forego his customary visit to Chicago that week and remain over Sunday in Springfield. He devoted the day to composing a long letter to Miss Greene, in which he described the situation in detail, and suggested that it would be well for her, if possible, to come down to Springfield on Monday and stay until the resolution had been adopted. He gave her, in closing, such pledges of his devotion to the cause of womankind that she could hardly resist any appeal he might make for her presence and assistance.

On Monday he wired, urging the necessity of her presence. Tuesday morning brought him a reply, thanking him, in behalf of women, for his disinterested devotion to their cause, assuring him of her own appreciation of his services, and saying that she would reach Springfield—Wednesday morning.

Meanwhile he had had no letter from Amelia, and he began to wonder at her silence. He was not only disappointed, but also piqued. He felt that his achievement deserved the promptest recognition from her, but he found a consolation, that grew in spite of him, in the thought that Maria Greene would soon be in Springfield, and to his heart he permitted Amelia's silence to justify him in a freer indulgence of attention to this fascinating woman lawyer.

Tuesday evening the crowd, that grows larger as the session nears its close, filled the lobby of the Leland. The night was warm, and to the heat of politics was suddenly added the heat of summer. Doors and windows were flung wide to the night, and the tall Egyptians, used as they were to the sultry atmospheres of southern Illinois, strode lazily about under their wide slouch hats with waistcoats open and cravats loosened, delighting in a new cause for chaffing the Chicago men, who had resumed their cus-

tomary complaints of the Springfield weather.

The smoke of cigars hung in
the air. The sound of many
voices, the ring of heavy laughter,
the shuffle of feet over the tiles,
the clang of the clerk's gong, the
incessant chitter of a telegraph in-
strument that sped news to Chicago over the *Courier's* private
wire, all these influences sur-
charged the heavy air with a nervous excitement that made men
speak quickly and their eyes glit-
ter under the brilliant lights of
countless electric bulbs. There
was in that atmosphere the play of
myriad hopes and ambitions, political, social, financial. Special
delegations of eminent lawyers,
leading citizens and prominent
capitalists were down from Chicago to look after certain measures of importance. Newspaper

correspondents hurried from group to group, gathering bits of information to be woven into their night's dispatches.

Late in the evening the governor came over from the mansion, and his coming stirred the throng with a new sensation. His secretary was by his side, and they mingled a while with the boys, as the governor called them, after the politician's manner. Half a dozen congressmen were there, thinking always of renomination. Over in one corner sat a United States senator, his high hat tilted back on his perspiring brow. A group of men had drawn their chairs about him. They laughed at his stories.

One was aware that the speaker's apartments upstairs were crowded. One could easily imagine it. The door of his inner room, as men came and went,

opening now and then, and giving
a glimpse of the speaker himself,
tired and worn under the strain
that would tell so sorely on him
before another week could bring
his labors and his powers and his
glories to an end.   Through all
that hotel that night, in lobby and
in barroom, on the stairs, in the
side halls and up and down in the
elevators, throbbed the fascination
of politics, which men play not so
much for its ends as for its means.

Morley was of this crowd,
moving from one group to another,
laughing and talking.   His heart
may have been a little sore at the
thought of Amelia's strange ne-
glect of him, but the soreness had
subsided until now it was but a
slight numbness which he could
forget at times, and when he did
think of it, it but gave him resolu-

tion to play the game more fiercely.

He knew that it was incumbent on him to make sure of the adoption of the resolution on the morrow. He had already spoken to the lieutenant governor and had promised of recognition. But he realized that it would be wise to make a little canvass, though he had no doubt that all was well, and that by the next night he could mingle with this crowd serene and happy in the thought that his work was done. Perhaps he might even spend the evening in the company of Maria Greene. His heart gave a little leap at this new and happy thought and if the remembrance of Amelia came back just at that instant, its obtrusion only made his eyes burn the brighter.

He found it pleasant as he threaded his way through the crowd to halt senators as he met them and say, "Well, the woman-suffrage resolution comes up to-morrow.   You'll be for it, of course?"

It gave him such a legislative and statesmanlike importance to do this. As he was going leisurely about this quest, testing some of the sensations of a parliamentary leader, Cowley, the correspondent of the *Courier* accosted him, and, showing his teeth in that odd smile of his, asked if he cared to say anything about the resolution.

"Only that it comes up as a special order in the morning, and that I have no doubt whatever of its adoption by the Senate."

"Have you assurances from—"

"From everybody, and every assurance," said Morley. "They're all for it. Come and have a cigar."

They went over to the cigar stand, and when Cowley had lit his cigar, he said, "Let's go out for a little walk. I might be able to tell you something that will interest you."

IX

MORLEY was glad enough of a breath of the evening air, and they went down the steps to the sidewalk. Along the curbstone many men had placed chairs and in these cool and quiet eddies of the brawling stream of politics they joked and laughed peacefully. Sixth Street stretched away dark and inviting. Morley and Cowley turned southward and strolled along companionably. The air was delicious after the blaze of the hotel. The black shade of a moonless night was restful.

"I've just got hold of a story," began Cowley, after they had enjoyed the night for a moment in silence, "which you ought to know." He spoke from the detached standpoint of a newspaperman.

"What is it?" asked Morley

"Porter and Braidwood are against your resolution." Cowley spoke these names in a tone that told how futile any opposition would be. "And Wright and his fellows are against it, too," he added.

"Nonsense," said Morley

"Well, you'll see," replied Cowley.

"But they told me—"

"Oh, well, that's all right. They've changed in the last day or two."

"Why?"

"Well, they say it's risky from a party standpoint. They think they already have all the load they want to carry in the fall campaign. Besides, they—"

"What?"

"They say there's no demand for such a radical step, and so see no reason for taking it."

"No demand for it?"

"No, on the contrary," Cowley halted an instant and in his palm sheltered a lighted match for his extinguished cigar. "On the contrary, there's a lot of people against it."

"Since when?"

"They've been getting letters in the last few days—they've just been pouring in on 'em—and they're from women, too."

"From women?"

"Yes, from women. The first ladies in the land." Cowley spoke with a sneer.

Morley laughed.

Howard Chandler Christy, 1902

"All right," said Cowley in the careless tone of one who has discharged a duty. "Wait till you see Mrs. Overman Hodge-Lathrop land in here tomorrow."

"Mrs. Overman Hodge-Lathrop?" Morley stopped still in the middle of the sidewalk and turned in surprise and fear to Cowley.

Cowley enjoyed the little sensation he had produced. "Yes, she's coming down on the Alton tonight. And she's bringing some of her crowd with her. The women's clubs are all stirred up about the matter."

Morley was silent for a moment, then he wheeled suddenly and said, "Well, I'm much obliged to you, Cowley, but I'd better be getting back to the hotel."

"It may not be serious after all," Cowley said with tardy reassurance, "but there's danger, and I thought I'd let you know. I'm sending a pretty good story in to-night about it. They'll cover the Chicago end from the office."

"But they were all for it," Morley muttered.

"You know they never took the thing very seriously. Of course they passed it in the House just to line up old man Ames for the apportionment bill. They didn't think it would amount to anything."

"Yes, I know—but Maria Burley Greene—"

"Well, she's a pretty woman. That's all."

"You bet she is," said Morley, "and she'll be down here again tomorrow, too."

"Will she?" said Cowley eagerly, with his strange smile.

"Yes—but, look here, Charlie," Morley exclaimed, "don't you go mixing me up with her, now, understand?"

"Oh, I understand," said Cowley, and he laughed significantly.

When Morley reached the hotel he set to work in earnest. He tramped about half the night, until he had seen every senator who could be found. He noted a change in them. If he did not find them hostile he found many of them shy and reluctant. But when he went to his room he had enough promises to allay his fears and to restore, in a measure, his confidence, and he fell asleep thinking of Maria Greene, happy in the thought that she would be there with her charms to offset the social influence of Mrs. Overman Hodge-Lathrop.

X

MORLEY went down to breakfast the next morning wearing the new summer clothes his tailor had sent to him from Chicago the day before. He had a flower in his buttonhole—a red rose showing his colors for the final triumphant day.

The rotunda of the hotel, swept of the litter of the night before, was clean and cool, and the morning air of a perfect day came in refreshingly at the open doors. The farmer members, confirmed in the habit of early rising, were already sauntering aimlessly about, but otherwise statesmen still

109

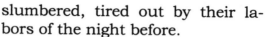

slumbered, tired out by their labors of the night before.

Morley, in the nervous excitement which arouses one at the
dawn of any day that is to be big
with events, had risen earlier than
was his wont. He hastened in to
the dining room, and there, at the
first table his eye alighted on, sat
Maria Burley Greene. She saw
him at once, for she faced the
door, and she greeted him with a
brilliant smile. With springing
step he rushed toward her, both
hands extended in his eagerness.
She half rose to take them. Their
greeting silenced the early break-
fasters for an instant. Then he sat
down opposite her and leaned over
with a radiant face as near to her
as might be, considering the width
of tablecloth and the breakfast
things between.

110

"And so you're here at last!" he exclaimed.

His eyes quickly took in her toilet. Remarkably fresh it was, though it had been made on the Springfield sleeper. It gave none of those evidences of being but the late flowering of a toilet that had been made the night before, as do the toilets of some ladies under similar circumstances. She wore this morning a suit of brown, tailored faultlessly to every flat seam, and a little turban to match it. Beside her plate lay her veil, her gloves, and a brass tagged key. And her face, clear and rosy in its rich beauty, was good to look upon. The waiter had just brought her strawberries.

"Send John to me," said Morley to the waiter. "I'll take my breakfast here. May I?" He lifted his eyes to Miss Greene's.

"Surely," said she, "we'll have much to discuss."

"And so you're here again at last," repeated Morley as if he had not already made the same observation. He laid, this time, perhaps a little more stress on the "at last." She must have noted that fact, for she blushed, red as the strawberries she began to turn over with a critically poised fork.

"And did you come down alone?" Morley went on.

"No, not exactly," said Miss Greene. Mrs. Overman Hodge-Lathrop, and I believe, several—"

"Mrs. Overman Hodge-Lathrop!"

"I think," said Miss Greene, "that she sits somewhere behind." There was a twinkle in the eyes she lifted for an instant from her berries.

113

Morley scanned the dining room. There was Mrs. Overman Hodge-Lathrop, in all her—and yes, beside her, sheltered snugly under he all-protecting wing, was Amelia Ansley! They were at a long table, Mrs. Overman Hodge-Lathrop at the head, and with them half a dozen women, severe, and most aggressively respectable. They sat—all of them—erect, pecking at their food with a distrust that was not so much a material caution as a spiritual evidence of their superiority to most of the things with which they were thrust in contact every day. Their hats scarcely trembled, such was the immense propriety of their attitudes. They did not bend at all, even to the cream.

Morley, who was taking all this in at a glance, saw that Mrs. Overman Hodge-Lathrop was severer than he had ever imagined it possible for women to be—even such a woman as she. He would not have been surprised had he suddenly been told that her name had acquired another hyphen. Certainly her dignity had been re-hyphenated. There she sat, with her broad shoulders and ample bust, her arms jeopardizing the sleeves of her jacket.

It was the most impressive breakfast table he had ever seen. It might have given him a vision of the future, when he should have secured for women all their civil and political rights, and the nation had progressed to female lieutenant generals, who would be forced at times to dine in public with their staffs. But he had no such vision, of course. The very spiritual aversion of those women to

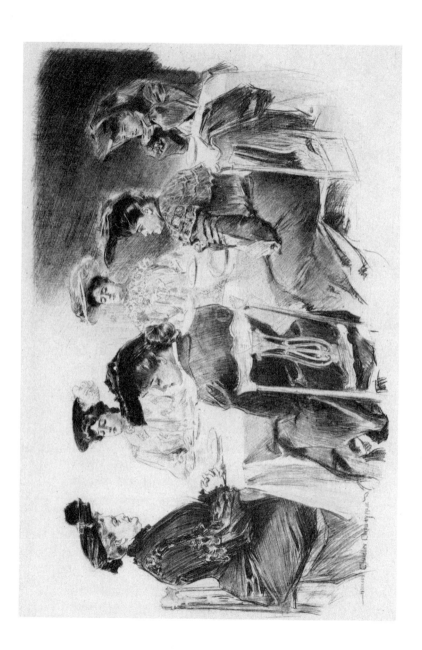

such a thought would have prevented it.

In point of fact, his regard in an instant had ceased to be general and had become specific, having Amelia for its objective. She sat on the right of her commander, a rather timid aide. And she seemed spiritually to snuggle more closely under her protecting shadow with each passing moment. She seemed to be half frightened, and had the look of a little girl who is about to cry. Her gray figure, with its hat of violets above her dark hair, was, on the instant, half-pathetic to Morley. She sat facing him, her face downcast.

There was no conversation at that table. It was to be seen at a glance indeed that among those ladies there would be need for none, all things having been prearranged for them. Morley noted that Amelia seemed to him more dainty, more fragile than she had ever been before, and his heart surged out toward her. Then she raised her eyes slowly, and held him, until from their depths she stabbed with one swift glance, a glance full of all accusation, indictment and reproach. The stab went to his heart with a pain that made him exclaim. Then perceiving that the complicating moments were flying, he rose hastily, and with half an apology to Miss Greene, he rushed across the dining room.

XI

NONE of the ladies relaxed at Morley's approach, Mrs. Overman Hodge-Lathrop least of all. On the contrary, she seemed to swell into proportions that were colossal and terrifying, and when Morley came within her sphere of influence his manner at once subdued itself into an apology.

"Why, Amelia—Mrs. Overman Hodge-Lathrop!" he cried, "and Mrs. Standish, Mrs. Barbourton, Mrs. Trales, Mrs. Langdon—how do you do?"

He went, of course, straight to Mrs. Overman Hodge-Lathrop's side, the side that sheltered

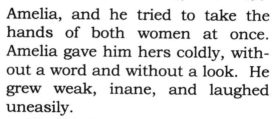

Amelia, and he tried to take the hands of both women at once. Amelia gave him hers coldly, without a word and without a look. He grew weak, inane, and laughed uneasily.

"Delightful morning," he said, "this country air down here is—"

"Morley," said Mrs. Overman Hodge-Lathrop, severely, "take that seat at the foot of the table."

He obeyed, meekly. The ladies, he thought, from the rustle of their skirts, withdrew themselves subtly. The only glances they vouchsafed him were sidelong and disapproving. He found it impossible to speak, and so waited. He could not recall having experienced similar sensations since those menacing occasions of boyhood when he had been sent to the library to await his father's coming.

120

"Delightful morning, indeed!" Mrs. Overman Hodge-Lathrop said, in her most select tones. "Delightful morning to bring us poor old ladies down into the country!"

"I bring you down?" Morley asked incredulously.

"Morley," she said, "I don't wish to have one word from you, not one. Do you understand? Your talent for speech has caused trouble enough as it is. Lucky we shall be if we can undo the half of it!"

Morley shrank.

"Morley Vernon," Mrs. Overman Hodge-Lathrop continued, "do you know what I have a notion to do?"

"No, Mrs. Overman Hodge-Lathrop," he said in a very little voice.

"Well, sir, I've a notion to give you a good spanking."

121

Morley shot a glance at her.

"Oh, you needn't look, sir, " she continued, "you needn't look! It wouldn't be the first time, as you well know—and it isn't so many years ago—and I have your mother's full permission, too."

The chain of ladylike sympathy that passed about the table at this declaration was broken only when its ends converged on Morley. Even then they seemed to pinch him.

"Your poor, dear mother," Mrs. Overman Hodge-Lathrop went on, "insisted, indeed, on coming down herself, but I knew she could never stand such a trip. I told her," and here Mrs. Overman Hodge-Lathrop paused for an instant, "I told her that I thought *I* could manage."

There was a vast significance in this speech.

122

The waiter had brought the substantials to the ladies, and Mrs. Overman Hodge-Lathrop began eating determinedly.

"It was, of course, just what I had always predicted," she went on, in a staccato that was timed by the rise of her fork to her lips, "I knew that politics would inevitably corrupt you, soon or late. And now it has brought you to this."

"To what?" asked Morley, suddenly growing bold and reckless. Amelia had not given him one glance. She was picking at her eggs.

Mrs. Overman Hodge-Lathrop, raising her gold glasses and setting them aristocratically on the bridge of her nose, fixed her eyes on Morley.

"Morley," she said, "we know. We have heard and we have read.

123

The Chicago press is an institution that, fortunately, still survives in these iconoclastic days. You know very well, of course, what I mean. Please do not compel me to go into the revolting particulars." She took her glasses down from her nose, as if that officially terminated the matter.

"But really, Mrs. Overman Hodge-Lathrop," said Morley. He was growing angry, and then, too, he was conscious somehow that Miss Greene was looking at him.

His waiter, John, timidly approached with a glance at the awful presence of Mrs. Overman Hodge-Lathrop, and said, "Yo' breakfas', Senator, is getting' col'."

"That may wait," said Mrs. Overman Hodge-Lathrop, and John sprang back out of range.

Morley was determined, then, to have it out.

"Really, Mrs. Overman Hodge-Lathrop, jesting aside—"

"Jesting!" cried Mrs. Overman Hodge-Lathrop, "Jesting! Indeed, my boy, this is quite a serious business!" She tapped with her forefinger.

"Well, then, all right," said Morley, "I don't know what I've done. All I have done has been to champion a measure—and I may add, without boasting, I hope, with some success—all I have done has been to champion a measure which was to benefit your sex, to secure your rights, to—"

"Morley!" Mrs. Overman Hodge-Lathrop cut him short. "Morley, have you indeed fallen so low? It is incomprehensible to me, that a young man who had the mother you have, who had the advantages you have had, who was born and

bred as you were, should so easily
have lost his respect for women!"

"Lost my respect for women!"
cried Morley, and then he laughed.
"Now, Mrs. Overman Hodge-
Lathrop," he went on with a shade
of irritation in his tone, "this is too
much!"

Mrs. Overman Hodge-Lathrop
was calm.

"Have you shown her any respect?" she went on. "Have you
not, on the contrary said and done
everything you could to drag her
down from her exalted station, to
pull her to the earth, to bring her
to a level with men, to make her
soil herself with politics, by
scheming and voting and caucus-
ing and buttonholing and wire-
pulling? You would have her de-
grade and unsex herself by going
to the poll, to caucuses and conventions. You would have her, no

126

doubt, in time, lobbying for and against measures in the council chamber and the legislature."

Mrs. Overman Hodge-Lathrop paused and lifted her gold eyeglasses once more to the bridge of her high, aristocratic nose.

"Is it that kind of women you have been brought up with, Morley? Do we look like that sort? Glance around this table—do we look like that sort of women?"

The ladies stiffened haughtily, disdainfully, under the impending inspection, knowing full well how easily they would pass muster.

"And, if that were not enough," Mrs. Overman Hodge-Lathrop went on inexorably, "we come here to plead with you and find you hobnobbing with that mannish thing, that *female* lawyer!"

She spoke the word *female* as if it conveyed some distinct idea of reproach. She was probing another chop with her fork. She had sent the pot of coffee back to the kitchen, ordering the waiter to tell the cook that she was accustomed to drink her coffee hot.

"And now, Morley Vernon, listen to me," she said, as if he were about to hear the conclusion of the whole matter. "If you have any spark of honor left in you, you will undo what you have already done. This resolution must be defeated in the Senate today. I am down here to see that it is done. We go to the State House after breakfast, and these ladies will assist me in laying before each member of the Senate this matter in its true and exact light. As for our rights," she paused and looked at him fixedly, "as for our rights, I think we are perfectly capable of preserving them."

Her look put that question beyond all dispute.

"And now," she resumed, "you
would better take a little breakfast
yourself. You look as if you
needed strength."

Morley rose. He stood for an
instant looking at Amelia, but she
glanced at him only casually.

"I suppose, Amelia, I shall see
you later in the morning?"

"I suppose so, Mr. Vernon," she
said. "But pray do not let me keep
you from rejoining your compan-
ion." She was quite airy, and
lifted her coffee cup with one little
finger quirked up higher than he
had ever seen it before.

He went back to where Miss
Greene sat, and where his breakfast lay.

"My goodness!" he said, seating
himself. "I've had a time!"

"I should imagine so," said Miss Greene.

She was just touching her napkin to her lips with a final air. She carefully pushed back her chair, and rose from the table.

"I beg your pardon," he stammered, getting up himself, "I'll see you after breakfast.

Miss Greene bowed. Then she left the dining room.

XII

MORLEY VERNON came out of the dining room in a temper far different from that he had worn when he went in. His breakfast, after so many vicissitudes, was sure to be a failure, though John, striving against fate, had tried to restore the repast to its original excellence by replacing each dish with a fresh one. He affected a heroic cheerfulness, too, but the cheer was hollow, for his experience of men and of breakfasts must have taught him that such disasters can never be repaired.

Morley, however, had heavier things on his mind. In his new

position as knight-errant of Illinois womankind, he had looked forward to this day as the one of triumph. Now, at its beginning, he found himself with two offended women on his hands, and two hopelessly irreconcilable mistresses to serve. He began to see that the lot of a constructive statesman is trying. He would never criticize leaders again.

The lobby of the hotel was filling rapidly, and men with their hair still damp from the morning combing were passing into the breakfast room with newspapers in their hands. In the center of the lobby, however, he saw a group of senators, and out of the middle of the group rose a dark bonnet. The flowers on the bonnet bobbed now and then decisively. Around it were clustered other

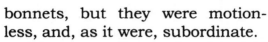

bonnets, but they were motionless, and, as it were, subordinate.

"Can you tell me who that is?" asked Brooks of Alexander, jerking his thumb at the group.

"Yes," said Morley, "That's General Hodge-Lathrop. She's on her way to the front to assume command."

"Oh!" said Brooks. "I saw something in the papers—" And he went away, reading as he walked.

Morley looked everywhere for Miss Greene, but he could not find her. The porter at the Capitol Avenue entrance told him that she had driven over to the State House a few minutes before. Morley was seized by an impulse to follow, but he remembered Amelia. He could not let matters go on thus between them. If only Mrs. Overman Hodge-Lathrop were not in command. If he could get Amelia

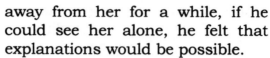

away from her for a while, if he could see her alone, he felt that explanations would be possible.

He looked at his watch. It was half-past nine. The Senate would not be reached before half-past ten at any rate. And so he determined to brave Mrs. Overman Hodge-Lathrop again. He turned back into the lobby. There she was, hobnobbing with men. She did not pass from group to group, after the manner of any other lobbyist, but by some coercion he wished he might be master of, she drew them unerringly to her side. Now she had Braidwood, the leader of the House, and chairman of the steering committee, and Porter, the leader of the Senate. She appeared to be giving them instructions.

She had set her committee on less important games. The ladies were scattered over the rotunda, each talking to a little set of men. When Mrs. Overman Hodge-Lathrop saw Morley coming, she turned from Braidwood and Porter and stood awaiting him. Strangely enough Braidwood and Porter stayed where they were, as if she had put them there. And Morley reflected that he had never known them, as doubtless no one else had ever known them, to do such a thing as that before.

"Where's Amelia?" he asked before she could speak.

"I have sent her upstairs," said Mrs. Overman Hodge-Lathrop, "poor child!"

Morley wondered why "poor child."

"It's really too bad," Mrs. Overman Hodge-Lathrop continued.

"What is too bad?" demanded Morley. He had grown sulky.

135

Mrs. Overman Hodge-Lathrop looked at him pityingly.

"Morley," she said in a vast solemn tone that came slowly up from her great stays, "I can make allowances, of course. I know something of the nature of man. I will admit that that Greene woman is remarkably handsome, and of her cleverness there can be no doubt. I don't altogether blame you."

She paused that Morley might comprehend to the fullest her marvelous magnanimity.

"But at the same time it has been hard on poor little Amelia. I saw no other way than to bring her down. You must go to her at once."

She turned toward Braidwood and Porter, still standing where she had left them.

"When you have done, I'll see you with reference to this miserable resolution. But that can wait till we are at the Capitol. This other matter comes first, of course."

She smiled with a fat sweetness.

"And Morley," she said, "order two carriages for us at ten o'clock. You may drive to the Capitol with us."

And she went away.

Morley ordered the carriages, and in turning the whole matter over in his mind he came to the conclusion that he must deal with these complications one at a time. Miss Greene, as events now had shaped themselves, would have to wait until he got over to the State House.

137

XIII

MORLEY found Amelia in one of the hotel parlors, seated on a sofa by a window. She was resting her chin in her hand and looking down into Capitol Avenue.

"Amelia," he said, bending over her. "What is it? Tell me."

He sat down beside her, and sought to engage one of her hands in his own, but she withdrew it, and pressed it with the other and the handkerchief in both, to her lips and chin. Morley glanced about the respectable parlors, maintained in instant readiness for anybody that might happen along with his little comedy or his

138

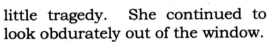

little tragedy. She continued to look obdurately out of the window.

"Amelia," he said, "aren't you going to speak to me? Tell me what I have done."

Still there came no answer. He sat back on the sofa helplessly.

"Well," he said, "I don't know what it all means. I've tried to fathom it in the last hour, but it's too deep for me. I give it up." He flung out his hands to illustrate his abandonment.

"God knows," he suddenly exclaimed, "I was only trying to do something worthy—for your sake!"

"Please don't swear, Morley," Amelia said.

He looked up swiftly.

"Well—" he began explosively, but he didn't continue. He relapsed into a moody silence. He stretched his legs out before him in an ungainly attitude, with his

139

Howard Chandler Christy–1905

hands plunged deep in his trousers' pockets. Then he knitted his brows and tried to think.

"I suppose," he said, as if he were thinking aloud, "that you expect some explanation, some apology."

"Oh, not at all," she said lightly, in the most musical tone she could command.

"Very well," he said, "I wouldn't know where to begin if you did. I'm sure I'm not aware of having committed—"

She began to hum softly, to herself, some tuneless air. He remembered that it was a way she had when she was angry. It was intended to show the last and utmost personal unconcern. In such circumstances the tune was apt to be an improvisation and was never melodious. Sometimes it made her easier to deal with,

141

sometimes harder. He could never
tell.

"I don't exactly see what we are
here for," he ventured, stealing a
look at her. She had no reply. He
fidgeted a moment and then began
drumming with his fingers on the
arm of the sofa.

"Please don't do that," she said.

He stopped suddenly. "If you
would be good enough, *kind*
enough," he said it sarcastically,
"to indicate, to suggest even, what
I am to do—to say."

"I'm sure I can't," she said.
"You came. I presumed you had
something to say to me."

"Well, I have something to say
to you," Morley went on impetu-
ously. "Why didn't you answer my
letters? Why have you treated me
this way? That's what I want to
know."

He leaned toward her. He was conscious of two emotions, two passions, struggling within him, one of anger, the other of love, and strangely enough they had a striking similarity in their effect upon him. He felt like reproaching, yet he knew that was not the way, and he made a desperate struggle to conquer himself.

He tried to look into her face, but she only turned farther away from him.

"I've spent the most miserable week I ever knew, doomed to stay here, unable to get away to go to you, and with this fight on my hands!"

"You seemed to be having a fairly good time," she observed.

"Now, Amelia, look here," said Morley, "let's not act like children any longer. Let's not have anything so foolish and little between us."

His tone made his words a plea, but it plainly had no effect upon her, for she did not answer. They sat there in silence.

"Why didn't you write?" Morley demanded after a little while. He looked at her, and she straightened up and her eyes flashed.

"Why didn't I write!" she exclaimed. "What was I to write, pray? Were not your letters full of this odious Maria Burlaps Greene? And as if that were not enough, weren't the papers full of you two? And that speech—oh, that speech—that Portia and Helen, and 'I fill this cup to one made up,' ah, it was sickening!" She turned away.

"But, darling," Morley cried, "listen—you misunderstood—I

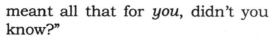

meant all that for *you*, didn't you know?"

She stirred.

"Didn't you see? Why, dearest, I thought that when you read the papers you'd be the proudest girl alive!"

Her lip curled. "I read the papers," she paused, adding significantly, "this once, anyway."

"Well, you certainly don't intend to hold me responsible for what the papers say, do you?"

She resumed her old attitude, her elbow on the arm of the sofa, her chin in her hand, and looked out the window. And she began to hum again.

"And then," he pressed on, "to come down here and not even let me know. Why you even called me *Mister* Vernon when I came into the dining room.

"Yes," she replied, wheeling about. "I *saw* you come into the dining room this morning!" Her eyes grew dark and flashed.

He regretted, on the instant."

"I saw you!" she went on. "I saw you rush up to that Maria Burlaps Greene woman, and—oh, it was horrid!"

"Her name isn't Burlaps, dear," said Morley.

"How do you know her name, I'd like to know?" She put her hands to her face.

He saw her tears. "Amelia," he said masterfully, "if you don't stop that! Listen—we've got to get down to business."

She hastily brushed the tears from her eyes. She was humming once more, and tapping the toe of her boot on the carpet, though she was not tapping it in time to her tune.

"Why did you come down without letting me know?" Morley went on. But she remained silent.

"You might at least have given me—"

"Warning?" she said, with a keen inflection.

"Amelia!" he said, and his tone carried a rebuke.

"Well, I don't care!" she cried. "It's all true! You couldn't stay for my dinner, but you could come off down here and—"

She covered her face with her hands and burst suddenly into tears. Morley gazed at her in astonishment.

"Why, dearest!" he said leaning over, and trying to take her in his arms. She drew away from him, and sobbed. Morley glanced about the room helplessly. He pleaded with her, but she would not listen. Neither would she be comforted,

147

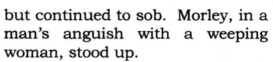

but continued to sob. Morley, in a man's anguish with a weeping woman, stood up.

"Amelia! Amelia!" He bent over her and spoke firmly. "You must not! Listen to me! We must go over to—"

Suddenly he stood erect and jerked out his watch.

"Heavens!" he cried. "It's half-past ten!"

She tried to control herself then, and sitting up, began to wipe her eyes.

"Sweetheart," he said, "I must go now. I should have been in the Senate at ten o'clock. I hate to leave you, but I'll explain everything when I get back."

He waited an instant, then he went on.

"Aren't you going to say 'Good by?'"

Amelia got up.

"I'll go, too," she said. She was still catching little sobs in her throat now and then. Vernon looked at her in some surprise.

"Why—" he began, incredulously.

She must have divined his surprise.

"I have to help Mrs. Overman Hodge-Lathrop," she said, as if in explanation. "But, of course, I hate to bother you."

"Oh, nonsense, dearest," he said, impatiently. "Come on. Let's start."

"But I can't go looking this way," she said. She walked across the room, and standing before a mirror, wiped her eyes carefully, then arranged her hat and her veil.

"Would anybody know?" she asked, facing about for his inspection.

"Never—come on."

They went out, and down the elevator. When they reached the entrance, Morley looked up and down the street, but there was no carriage in sight. The street was quiet and the hotel wore an air of desertion, telling that all the political activity of Illinois had been transferred to the State House. Morley looked around the corner, but the old hack that always stood there was not at its post.

"We'll have to walk," he said. "It'll take too long for them to get a carriage around for us. It's only a few blocks, anyway. The air will do you good."

As they set forth in the bright morning sun they were calmer, and having come out into public view, for the time being they dropped their differences and their misunderstandings, and began to

150

talk in their common, ordinary fashion.

"Did Mrs. Overman Hodge-Lathrop ask you to change me on the Ames Amendment?" Morley asked her.

"The what?"

"The Ames Amendment. That's the woman-suffrage measure."

"No, do her justice. She didn't."

"What then?"

"She said she wanted me to work against it, that's all."

"Didn't she say anything about asking *me* not to vote for it?"

"Well, yes. But I told her—"

"What?"

"That I wouldn't try to influence you in the least."

Morley made no reply.

"No," she went on, "I'm to work against it, of course."

151

They were silent then, till suddenly she appealed to him.

"Oh, Morley, I've got to ask strange men, men I never met, to vote against it! How am I ever?"

She shuddered.

"It's all very strange," Morley said.

XIV

THEY walked briskly down the sloping street under the railroad bridge and then up the little hill whereon sits the Capitol of Illinois. They could see the big flag high up on the dome standing out in the prairie wind, and the little flags on the House wing and the Senate wing whipping joyously, sprightly symbols of the sitting of both houses.

Now and then they heard cheers from the House wing, where the legislative riot that ends a session was already beginning. They passed into the dark and cold corridors of the State House, then up to the third floor, where

153

members and messenger boys, correspondents and pageboys, rushed always across from one house to the other, swinging hurriedly around the brass railing of the rotunda. It seemed that the tide of legislative life was just then setting in toward the Senate.

"Oh, Morley," whispered Amelia, forgetting his offense, and clinging close to him, "I can't go in there, really I can't."

"Nonsense," said Morley, "come on. I'll deliver you to Mrs. Hodge-Lathrop in a minute. Then you'll be perfectly safe. Besides, you have your lobbying to do."

They reached the Senate entrance, and the doorkeeper, seeing a senator, opened a way through the crowd for their passage. There was confusion everywhere, the nervous and excited hum of voices from the floor, from the vestibule, from the galleries, from all around. And just as they stepped up to the raised floor whereon the desks of senators are placed, the gavel fell, and stillness with it. They saw the lieutenant governor leaning over his desk, studying a slip of paper he held in his hand.

"On this question," he said, "the yeas are thirty and the nays are seventeen. And two-thirds of the members-elect having failed to vote in the affirmative, the resolution is lost."

Morley stood transfixed. The whole thing was borne in upon him. He saw Mrs. Overman Hodge-Lathrop, and the expression of calm and lofty satisfaction that had settled on her face told him that it was the Ames Amendment that had been lost. But some new thought seemed to strike her, for when Senator Porter

155

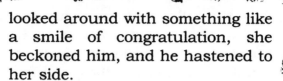

looked around with something like a smile of congratulation, she beckoned him, and he hastened to her side.

"Move to reconsider and to lay on the table," she said, and with a look of admiration he turned and made the motion. It was put, it was carried of course, and the amendment was lost irrevocably.

"Well, that's attended to," said Mrs. Overman Hodge-Lathrop. "Ah, Morley," she said calmly, "you here? And Amelia?"

"She's here," he said, "and I—I didn't get here on time!" The shame and mortification on his face were pitiable, though they could not have touched Mrs. Overman Hodge-Lathrop's heart.

"And I didn't get here on time," he repeated ruefully.

"Why, my dear boy," said Mrs. Overman Hodge-Lathrop, "I didn't intend that you should."

He looked at her fiercely, angrily. "So that was the game, was it? He whirled, with another fierce look for Amelia.

"That was the game, yes, Morley," said Mrs. Overman Hodge-Lathrop, "but you needn't look at Amelia so—she was utterly innocent, the dear little thing."

Amelia came up. She had seen Morley's expression.

"What is it—what has happened?" she asked naively.

"Well, I got here too late, that's all," said Morley. "I was detained, and Mrs. Hodge-Lathrop has just now kindly told me that she had arranged that I should be. I'm ruined, that's all. I'm lost."

"No, Morley," said Mrs. Hodge-Lathrop, "you're saved. You're

157

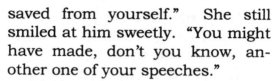

saved from yourself." She still
smiled at him sweetly. "You might
have made, don't you know, another one of your speeches."

Morley bit his lip and walked
away. He encountered Martin, but
could only look at him helplessly.
Martin returned his look with one
of surprise.

"You here?" he said.

"Well, yes," replied Morley. "At
last—too late, it seems."

The surprise had not left Martin's face. To it was now added a
perplexity.

"If we'd known," said Martin,
"but we thought that is, we heard
that you had ducked."

Morley shook his head as with
a pain that would not let him
speak. He was looking disconso-
lately across the chamber to where
Miss Greene stood talking with
Bull Burns. As in a dream, he

heard Mrs. Overman Hodge-Lathrop.

"Ah, there is that Greene woman!"

Mrs. Overman Hodge-Lathrop was lifting her gold glasses again. Morley was wondering how he was going to face the Greene woman. But at Mrs. Overman Hodge-Lathrop's words an idea came to him.

"I'll go bring her and introduce her," he said. He bolted away and went toward her. She was cold and distant. Fortunately, Burns fled at his approach.

"Can you forgive me?" he asked. "I'll explain it all in an instant."

"And how?" she asked with a chill in her tone.

"Have you ever met Mrs. Overman Hodge-Lathrop?" he asked significantly.

159

"No," she answered.

"Then permit me," he said. She went with him. Mrs. Overman Hodge-Lathrop had withdrawn her delegation to the rear of the chamber, and there awaited Morley's return.

"Mrs. Overman Hodge-Lathrop, permit me to present Miss Greene. Miss Ansley, Miss Greene." And so on, in the order of relative rank, he introduced her to the other ladies.

Mrs. Overman Hodge-Lathrop extended her hand officially. Miss Greene took it with a smile.

"I am very glad," she said, "to meet Mrs.—Mrs.—ah, pardon, me, but what was the name?"

"Mrs. Overman Hodge-Lathrop," Morley said.

"Ah, Mrs. Lathrop."

Mrs. Overman Hodge-Lathrop seemed to swell.

"You have a charming little city here, Mrs. Lathrop. We poor Chicagoans love to get down into the country once in a while, you know."

Mrs. Overman Hodge-Lathrop reared back a little.

"N—no doubt," she stammered. "I have always found Springfield charming, as well."

Miss Greene feigned surprise, and affected a look of perplexity. Morley withdrew a step, and with his chin in his hand looked on out of eyes that gloated. The other women in the party exchanged glances of horror and wrath. Mrs. Barbourton, for her part, seemed unable to endure it.

"Mrs. Overman Hodge-Lathrop lives in *Chicago*," she interjected.

"Oh!" cried Miss Greene. "Is it possible? How very strange that

161

one could live in the city all one's life and yet not have heard!"

"Not so very strange, I fancy," said Mrs. Overman Hodge-Lathrop. "One's circle is apt to be so far removed."

"Yes?" said Miss Greene, with that rising inflection. "Then you cannot have lived in Chicago long?"

"All my life!" snapped Mrs. Overman Hodge-Lathrop.

"So long as that?" asked Miss Greene, her eyes wide with incredulity. Mrs. Overman Hodge-Lathrop actually colored.

Miss Greene continued. "You are enjoying your visit to Springfield, I trust? You have seen the Lincoln Monument and the Homestead? How very interesting they must be! And the Legislature offers novelty. Don't you find it so?" She gathered her skirts as if to

162

withdraw. But Mrs. Overman Hodge-Lathrop achieved a smile.

"We have not enjoyed the pleasures of sight-seeing. On the contrary, we came to appear before the Senate."

Miss Greene surveyed her critically, with that look in which one woman inspects another woman's attire. She then extended her critical scrutiny to the dress of the others.

"To be sure!" she said. "I should have known."

The ladies again exchanged glances. Mrs. Barbourton plainly could not bear that their position should be ambiguous. She doubtless had her little vainglorious wish to have their success known.

"Mrs. Overman Hodge-Lathrop came down to appear in opposition to the woman's-rights resolu-

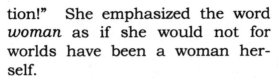

tion!" She emphasized the word *woman* as if she would not for worlds have been a woman herself.

"Indeed!" exclaimed Miss Greene. "I am sure her appearance must have been a very convincing argument." She gave her opponent another searching glance. Mrs. Overman Hodge-Lathrop was having difficulty in getting her breath.

"We have been having a taste of lobbying Miss Greene," she began, "and—"

"How unpleasant!" she said.

"You know, possibly," said Mrs. Overman Hodge-Lathrop, regaining something of her position.

"Indeed I do know," Miss Greene assented sweetly, "but where it is in the line of one's profession, duty obscures the unpleasantness. One cannot, you

165

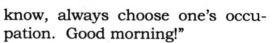

know, always choose one's occupation. Good morning!"

And catching her skirts, with a smile and a bow she left.

The successful lobbyists stood in silence a moment, looked one to another with wide and staring eyes. Then at last Mrs. Overman Hodge-Lathrop spoke.

"Morley," she said, "I do wish you could learn to discriminate in your introductions."

XV

JUST before dinner Amelia and Morley sat in the little waiting room of the hotel. Mrs. Overman Hodge-Lathrop and her ladies had gone up to the suite they had taken and were engaged in repairing the toilets their political labors of the morning had somewhat damaged. Amelia had completed her toilet more quickly than they and had joined Morley, waiting for her below.

They sat in the dim little room where Amelia could look across the corridor to the elevator, expecting every moment the coming of Mrs. Overman Hodge-Lathrop. Now that they found themselves

167

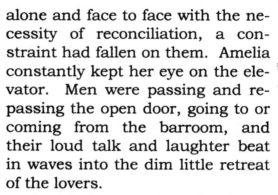

alone and face to face with the necessity of reconciliation, a constraint had fallen on them. Amelia constantly kept her eye on the elevator. Men were passing and repassing the open door, going to or coming from the barroom, and their loud talk and laughter beat in waves into the dim little retreat of the lovers.

As Morley sat there he imagined that all that talk was of him. More than all, that all that laughter was at him—though there was no more of either than there was every day when the legislators came over to the hotel for their big noon dinners. At last Amelia turned to him.

"You've got the blues, haven't you?" she said. It would seem that somehow he did her an injustice by having the blues.

"No," he answered.

168

"Then what's the matter?" she demanded.

Morley glanced at her, and his glance carried its own reproach.

"Oh!" she said, as if suddenly recalling a trivial incident. "Still worrying about that?"

"Well," Morley answered, "it has some seriousness for me."

Amelia, sitting properly erect, her hands folded in her lap, twisted about and faced him.

"You don't mean, Morley, that you are sorry it didn't pass, do you?"

"It puts me in rather an awkward position," he said. "I suppose you know that."

"I don't see how," Amelia replied.

"Well," Morley explained, 'to stand for a measure of that importance, and then at the final, critical moment, to fail—"

169

"Oh, I see!" said Amelia, moving away from him on the couch. "Of course, if you regret the *time*, if you'd rather have been over in the Senate than to have been with *me*—why, of course!" She gave a little deprecating laugh.

Morley leaned impulsively toward her.

"But, dear," he said, "you don't understand!"

"And after your begging me to come down to Springfield to see you!" Amelia said. Her eyes were fixed on the elevator, and just at that moment the car rushed down the shaft and swished itself to a stop just when, it seemed, it should have shattered itself to pieces at the bottom. The elevator boy clanged the iron door back, and Maria Greene stepped out.

"There she is now!" said Amelia, raising her head to see.

170

Miss Greene paused a moment to reply to the greeting of one of the politicians who stopped to speak to her.

Amelia's nose was elevated.

"And so that's the wonderful hair you all admire so much, is it?" she said.

"Well," replied Morley, almost defiantly, "don't you think it is rather exceptional hair?"

Amelia turned on him with a look of superior and pitying penetration.

"Does that shade deceive you?" she asked. She smiled disconcertingly, as she looked away again at Maria Greene. The woman lawyer was just leaving the politicians.

"And to think of wearing that hat with that hair!" Amelia went on. "Though of course," she added with deep meaning, "it may origi-

171

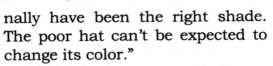

nally have been the right shade. The poor hat can't be expected to change its color."

Morley had no answer for her.

"I wonder what explanation she'll have for her defeat," said Amelia in a tone that could not conceal its spirit of triumph.

"I'm not worried about that," said Morley. "I'm more concerned about the explanation I'll have."

"Dearest!" exclaimed Amelia, swiftly laying her hand on his. Her tone had changed, and as she leaned toward him with the new tenderness that her new manner exhaled, Morley felt a change within himself, and his heart swelled.

"Dearest," she said, in a voice that hesitated before the idea of some necessary reparation, "are you really so badly disappointed?"

172

He looked at her, then suddenly he drew her into his arms, and she let her head rest for an instant on his shoulder. But only for an instant. Then she exclaimed and was erect and all propriety.

"You forget where we are, dear," she said.

"I don't care about that," he replied, and then glancing swiftly about in all directions, he kissed her.

"Morley!" she cried, and her cheeks went red, a new and happy red.

They sat there, looking at each other.

"You didn't consider, you didn't *really* consider her pretty, did you?" Amelia asked.

"Why, Amelia, what a question!"

173

"But you didn't? Don't evade, Morley."

"Oh well, now, she's not bad looking, exactly, but as for beauty—well, she's rather what I'd call handsome."

"Handsome!" Amelia exclaimed, drawing back.

"Why, yes. Don't you see, dear?" Morley was trying not to laugh. "Can't you see the distinction? We call *men* handsome, don't we? Not pretty, or anything like that. But women! Ah, women! Them we call, now and then, beautiful! And you, darling, you are beautiful!"

They were face to face again, both smiling radiantly. Then Amelia drew away, saying, "Morley, don't be ridiculous."

"But I'm dead in earnest, dear," he went on. "And I think you ought to make some sort of amends for all the misery you've caused me."

"You poor boy!" she said, with the pity that is part of a woman's triumph.

"I did it," he said, "just because I love you, and have learned in you what women are capable of, what they might do in politics—"

"In politics! Morley! Can you imagine me in politics? I thought you had a more exalted opinion of women. I thought you kept them on a higher plane."

"But you—" Morley laughed, and shook his head at the mystery of it, but did not go on.

"Why, Morley, would you want to see your mother or your sister or me, or even Mrs. Hodge-Lathrop in politics?"

"Well," he said, with a sudden and serious emphasis, "not Mrs. Hodge-Lathrop exactly. She'd be

176

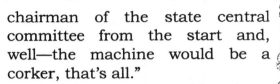

chairman of the state central committee from the start and, well—the machine would be a corker, that's all."

The elevator was rushing down again in its perilous descent, and when its door flew open they saw Mrs. Overman Hodge-Lathrop come out of the car. Morley rose hastily.

"There she is, " he said. "We mustn't keep her waiting."

Amelia rose, but she caught his hand and gave it a sudden pressure.

"But you haven't answered my question," she said, with a continuity of thought that was her final surprise for him. "Are you so very badly disappointed, after all?"

"Well, no," he said. "I don't think it would do. It would—well, it would complicate."

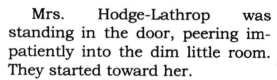

Mrs. Hodge-Lathrop was standing in the door, peering impatiently into the dim little room. They started toward her.

"Anyway, dear heart," Amelia whispered as they went, "remember this—that you did it all for me."

More

Great Lakes Romances®

For prices and availability, contact:
Bigwater Publishing
P.O. Box 177
Caledonia, MI 49316

Mackinac, First in the series of *Great Lakes Romances*® (Set at Grand Hotel, Mackinac Island, 1895.) Victoria Whitmore is no shy, retiring miss. When her father runs into money trouble, she heads to Mackinac Island to collect payment due from Grand Hotel for the furniture he's made. But dealing with Rand Bartlett, the hotel's manager, poses an unexpected challenge. Can Victoria succeed in finances without losing her heart?

The Captain and the Widow, Second in the series of *Great Lakes Romances*® (Set in South Haven, Michigan, 1897.) Lily Atwood Haynes is beautiful, intelligent, and alone at the helm of a shipping company at the tender age of twenty. Then Captain Hoyt Curtiss offers to help her navigate the choppy waters of widowhood. Together, can they keep a new shipping line—and romance—afloat?

Sweethearts of Sleeping Bear Bay, Third in the series of *Great Lakes Romances*® (Set in the Sleeping Bear Dune region of northern Michigan, 1898.) Mary Ellen Jenkins has successfully mastered the ever-changing shoals and swift currents of the Mississippi, but Lake Michigan poses a new set of challenges. Can she round the ever-dangerous Sleeping Bear Point in safety, or will the steamer—

and her heart—run aground under the influence of Thad Grant?

Charlotte of South Manitou Island Fourth in the series of *Great Lakes Romances®* (Set on South Manitou Island, Michigan, 1891-1898.) Charlotte Richards, fatherless at age eleven, thought she'd never smile again. But Seth Trevelyn, son of South Manitou Island's lightkeeper, makes it his mission to show her that life goes on, and so does true friendship. Together, they explore the World's Columbian Exposition in faraway Chicago where he saves her from a near-fatal fire. When he leaves the island to create a life of his own in Detroit, he realizes Charlotte is his one true love. Will his feelings be returned when she grows to womanhood?

Aurora of North Manitou Island Fifth in the series of *Great Lakes Romances®* (Set on North Manitou Island, Michigan, 1898-1899.) With her new husband, Harrison, lying helpless after an accident on stormy Lake Michigan, Aurora finds marriage far from the glorious romantic adventure she had anticipated. And when Serilda Anders appears out of his past to tend the light and nurse him to health, Aurora is certain her marriage is doomed. Maybe Cad Blackburn, with the ready wit and silver tongue, is the answer. But it isn't right to accept the safe harbor *he's* offering. Where is the light that will guide her though troubled waters?

Bridget of Cat's Head Point Sixth in the series of *Great Lakes Romances®* (Set in Traverse City and the Leelanau Peninsula of Michigan, 1899-1900.) When Bridget Richards leaves South Manitou Island to take up residence on Michigan's mainland, she suffers no lack of ardent suitors. Nat Trevelyn wants desperately to make her his bride and the mother of his two-year-old son. Attorney Kenton McCune showers her with gifts and rapt attention. And Erik Olson shows her the incomparable beauty and romance of a Leelanau summer. Who will finally win her heart?

Rosalie of Grand Traverse Bay Seventh in the series of *Great Lakes Romances®* (Set in Traverse City, Michigan, and

Winston-Salem, North Carolina, 1900.)
Soon after Rosalie Foxe arrives in Traverse City for the summer of 1900, she stands at the center of controversy. Her aunt and uncle are about to lose their confectionery shop, and Rosalie is being blamed. Can Kenton McCune, a handsome, Harvard-trained lawyer, prove her innocence and win her heart?

Isabelle's Inning Encore Edition #1 in the series of *Great Lakes Romances*® (Set in the heart of Great Lakes Country, 1903.) Born and raised in the heart of the Great Lakes, Isabelle Dorlon pays little attention to the baseball players patronizing her mother's rooming house—until Jack Weatherby moves in. He's determined to earn a position with the Erskine College Purple Stockings, and a place in her heart as well, but will his affections fade once he learns the truth about her humiliating flaw?

Jenny of L'Anse Bay Special Edition in the series of *Great Lakes Romances*® (Set in the Keweenaw Peninsula of Upper Michigan in 1867.) Eager to escape the fiery disaster that leaves her home in ashes, Jennifer Crawford sets out on an adventure to an Ojibway Mission on L'Anse Bay. In the wilderness, her affections grow for a native people very different from herself—especially for the chief's son, Hawk. Together, can they overcome the differences of their diverse cultures, and the harsh, deadly weather of the North Country?

Elizabeth of Saginaw Bay, Pioneer Edition in the series of *Great Lakes Romances*® (Set in the Saginaw Valley of Michigan, 1837.) The taste of wedding cake is still sweet in Elizabeth Morgan's mouth when she sets out with her bridegroom, Jacob, from York State for the new State of Michigan. But she isn't prepared for the untamed forest, crude lodgings, and dangerous diseases that await her there. Desperately, she seeks her way out of the forest that holds her captive, but God seems to have another plan for her future.

Sweet Clover—A Romance of the White City, Centennial Edition in the series of *Great Lakes Romances*® (Set in Chicago at the World's Columbian Exposition of

1893.) The Fair brought unmatched excitement and wonder to Chicago, inspiring this innocent romance by Clara Louise Burnham first published in 1894. In it, Clover strives to rebuild a lifelong friendship with Jack Van Tassel, a childhood playmate who's spent several years away from the home of his youth. But The Fair lures him back, and their long-lost friendship rekindles. Can true love conquer the years that have come between, or will betrayals of the past pose impenetrable barriers?

Unlikely Duet—Caledonia Chronicles— Part 1 in the series of *Great Lakes Romances®* (Set in Caledonia, Michigan, 1905.) Caroline Chappell practiced long and hard for her recital on the piano and organ in Caledonia's Methodist Episcopal Church. She even took up the trumpet and composed a duet to perform with Joshua Bolden, an ace trumpet player whom she'd long admired. Now, two days before the performance, it looks as if her recital will be upstaged by a hastily planned street concert by the Caledonia Band! Until Neal Taman steps in. With grace and ease, this urbane newcomer resolves the conflict between Caroline and the band. For this, she is grateful. But when he offers her comely cousin, Deborah, employment in a far-off city, suspicions arise. Is this supposedly overworked banker's son really seeking rest and a change of scene in the Village of Caledonia, or has he come to this small, rural community for some darker purpose?

Bigwater Classics™ **Series**

Great Lakes Christmas Classics, **A Collection of Short Stories, Poems, Illustrations, and Humor from Olden Days**—From the pages of the *Detroit Free Press* of 1903, the Traverse City *Morning Record* of 1900, and other turn-of-the-century sources come heart-warming, rib-tickling, eye-catching gems of Great Lakes Christmases past. So sit back, put your feet up, and prepare for a thoroughly entertaining escape to holidays of old!

Reader Survey—*Amelia*
Your opinion counts! Please fill out and
mail this form to:
Reader Survey
Bigwater Publishing
P.O. Box 177
Caledonia, MI 49316

Your
Name _____

Street _____

City,State,Zip _____

In return for your completed survey, we
will send you a bookmark and the latest
issue of our *Great Lakes Romances®
Newsletter*. If your name is not currently
on our mailing list, we will also include
four notepapers and envelopes of an his-
toric Great Lakes scene (while supplies
last).

1. Would you like to read more stories
    like *Amelia*, reprinted from turn-of-
    the-century romances?

    Yes____   No____

2. Where did you purchase this book? (If you borrowed it from a library, please give the name and location of the library.)

_____

3. What influenced your decision to read this book?

Front Cover____   First Page____

Back Cover Description____ Friends____

Publicity (please describe)_____

_____

4. Please indicate your age range:

Under 18____   25-34____   46-55____

18-24____   35-45____   Over 55____

If desired, include additional comments below.